Such a Time as This

Casey Bradford

SUCH A TIME AS THIS
Copyright © 2021 by Casey Bradford

Scripture quotations taken from The Holy Bible, New International Version®
NIV® Copyright © 1973 1978 1984 2011 by Biblica, Inc. TM Used by permission.
All rights reserved worldwide.

This is a work of fiction. Names, characters, places and incidents either are the
product of the author's imagination or are used fictitiously, and any resemblance
to actual persons, living or dead, businesses, companies, events, or locales is
entirely coincidental.

ISBN: 978-1-4866-2067-8
eBook ISBN: 978-1-4866-2068-5

Word Alive Press
119 De Baets Street Winnipeg, MB R2J 3R9
www.wordalivepress.ca

WORD ALIVE
—P R E S S—

Cataloguing in Publication information can be obtained from Library and
Archives Canada.

To Mom, for listening to all of my stories for so long.

Acknowledgements

I would like to thank everyone who helped with this book in some way. Thanks to my mom, who listened to my descriptions of characters and plot, and to my dad, who patiently answered my questions about WWII and helped fact check the book. Thanks to my two nanas, who both read it and were so encouraging, and thanks to my teachers, who read it as well. Thanks to Auntie Lori and Uncle Joe, who read it and offered so much helpful advice. Thanks to Mrs. O'Farrell for believing in it and encouraging me to pursue my dream of publishing. Thanks to Marina for being so helpful in the publishing process and answering my many questions about what steps to take next. And thank you to all of my family and friends who listened to me incessantly talk about Liesel as if she was a real person! I couldn't have done it without you!

"For if you remain silent at this time, relief and deliverance for the Jews will arise from another place, but you and your father's family will perish. And who knows but that you have come to your royal position for such a time as this?"
—Esther 4:14 (NIV)

Prologue

June 1980

"Grandma! Grandma!"

Liesel smiled as she looked at the little girl who tugged on her sleeve.

"Here," she said. "Come stand on this chair, Ruth, so you can see." She lifted the little girl up, then went back to rolling out the cookie dough.

In the background, music played quietly. The sun shone outside, and across the kitchen cupboards, a large banner proclaimed, "Happy Birthday, Charlotte!"

"Why are you making cookies?"

"Because it's your mom's birthday," Liesel replied.

"That's why we made her a big banner, right?"

"That's right," Liesel nodded. "It's always nice to celebrate the people we love."

"I love my mom!" Ruth bounced up and down from her place on the chair beside Liesel at the kitchen counter.

"Do you want to help me with the cookies?" Liesel offered.

"Yeah!"

Liesel held out a section of dough to the little girl, who took it eagerly, then frowned suddenly.

"What's wrong with your hands?" Ruth asked suddenly.

Liesel looked down. She hardly noticed the scars now, only when others pointed them out. They criss-crossed her hands in faint white lines, a visible reminder of long-ago hardships.

"They're scars, Ruth, from a long time ago," Liesel said.

"But how did you get them?" Ruth asked. She peered at Liesel's hands, studying the faint scars earnestly. Tentatively, she reached out a finger towards them.

Liesel put down the cookie dough she held and spread out her hands for Ruth's inspection.

"I got them from the war, honey," she said. "It's all right, you can touch them if you want." She smiled at Ruth, encouraging her to reach out and feel the scars.

Gently, Ruth traced the faint lines with her finger, then pulled back abruptly.

She lifted worried eyes to Liesel. "Did that hurt?"

Liesel chuckled. "No honey, it didn't. They're all healed now. It was a long time ago, so they don't hurt anymore."

"Oh." Ruth paused. "What's a war?" Her blue eyes were wide, but Liesel could see the confusion in them, and she wondered at how to explain war to a child.

"It's when people fight each other," Liesel said finally. "But this war was with the whole world. Everyone was fighting in it."

"Is that how you got those?" Ruth asked, pointing to Liesel's hands. "Did you fight?"

"No, honey," Liesel answered. "I spent two years in a camp, for people who didn't do what the government wanted."

"Oh." Ruth nodded, but Liesel knew she didn't understand, not now. Her young mind had never known the atrocities people can inflict on one another.

Satisfied, Ruth ran away from Liesel to where her mother was calling.

Liesel reached for the cookie cutter and began cutting out shapes, her hands working unconsciously. Her mind, however, went back, many years before to the reason for her scars.

Chapter One

July 1939

Liesel perched on a stool, staring out the window of the stable as she absently stroked her mare, Madchen's, nose.

In the distance, the lights of Berlin sparkled, showing off the city to all who passed. But it was here, at the von Schwarzkopf country manor, that Liesel felt most at home. For here, the trees waved gently as the breeze whispered through them. The green grass stretched for miles, stopping only as it reached the forest that bordered the von Schwarzkopf lands. And the sky that shone so blue was never blocked by dust that swirled up from the streets of Berlin.

Reluctantly, Liesel rose from the stool. It was late, and she knew she needed to get to bed. With a murmured goodbye to Madchen, she left the stable. Ahead of her loomed the manor house. A sprawling, castle-like structure, it was made of dark grey stone, trimmed with green.

Entering the house, Liesel handed her coat to a waiting maid. As she walked past the sitting room, she spotted her parents, Herman and Klara, were sitting, talking quietly, the rise and fall of their words reaching Liesel's ears, though she couldn't make out what they were saying. She continued down the hall, towards the grand staircase that dominated the large room at the end of the hall. At the top of the landing, she paused at the top to look down at the luxurious carpeting and elegant furnishings that made up the place she called home, if only for the summer, before entering her bedroom, where a sumptuous featherbed awaited her, the covers already turned down by a maid.

Liesel sighed deeply as she paused at the window. Thoughts of turning eighteen had plagued her mind for the last several weeks. The new age was like an adventure, making her tingle with excitement. Eighteen seemed like a magical gateway to adulthood, but yet, she couldn't help wonder what it would bring.

What will I do? I don't feel like a grown-up yet.

Liesel closed her eyes, imaging herself as a lady of eighteen. In her mind's eye, she swept around the ballroom in the arms of a handsome man. He whispered in her ear, and the diamonds in her ears flashed as she moved and caught the light.

Turning from the window, Liesel climbed into bed. In the distance, the lights of Berlin still sparkled.

• • •

The next morning a knock sounded on the front door while Liesel sat with her parents at breakfast. A maid hurried to answer it and soon returned, followed by a tall young man in a grey uniform. He was muscular, with a crisp, military crew cut for his blond hair. A nick from a recent shave marred his left cheek, drawing attention to the freckles that dusted the bridge of his nose across to his cheeks. Although he looked a man, his green eyes danced with all the carelessness of a boy at heart.

"Karl!" Liesel leapt up from the table and ran to embrace him. He absorbed the impact of her headlong rush, patting her back, and grinned at Herman and Klara, who smiled indulgently at their daughter's excitement.

"Karl, you never said you were coming!" Liesel released him, but didn't return to her seat at the table. Her blue eyes shone as she looked into his green ones.

Chuckling, Karl took her hand and led her to the table, where a fourth place setting had appeared, as if by magic. He seated her, then crossed to kiss Klara's cheek and shake Herman's hand.

"Now, Liesel," he said, taking a seat, "You know I could never stay away from you for too long. I've come to beg for an invitation to your birthday ball. I've heard it's to be the event of the season!"

"Hmm," Liesel tapped her chin with a finger, pretending to think, her eyebrow quirked. "All right," she said finally. "I suppose you're invited."

"Of course, you're invited," Klara said. "We planned on having you there."

"And don't you decide to stay home," Herman teased. "Who would keep an eye on the birthday girl here?"

"Father!"

"I must confess, however, that I'm also here on business," Karl said. "I have a message for you, Herr von Schwarzkopf."

"Certainly," Herman replied. "We'll go to my study after breakfast."

"Yes, let's not disturb such a lovely morning by speaking about business!" Liesel said.

A gentle breeze wafted through the dining room's open doors. Beyond, a green meadow stretched for miles

"Liesel dear, why don't you take Karl for a ride?" Klara suggested, catching her daughter's longing look towards the meadow. "After he speaks to your father, that is."

"I'd love to," Karl's face lit up as he nodded eagerly at Klara's suggestion. "If Liesel can spare a moment, of course," he teased.

Liesel tossed her shining blond hair haughtily, but then her face softened. "For you, always," she murmured.

"And how are your parents? I haven't seen Maria for quite some time," Klara said.

"They're well," Karl replied. "Father's been spending a great deal of time in Berlin, but Mother is at the estate."

"Tell her she must make time to come for a visit soon," Klara said.

"Does that invitation include me too?" he asked impishly.

"Of course," Liesel replied.

"Then I shall be sure to tell her."

As they finished eating, Herman stood from the table. "Shall we go to my study?" he asked Karl, who stood as well.

"Come to the stables when you're finished," Liesel called after him.

He turned and flashed her a grin, and then he was gone, his back ruler straight.

• • •

Karl hurried down the path to the stables. Ahead of him, he could see Liesel, dressed in a trim blue riding outfit, leading a tall chestnut mare out of the stable. She walked gracefully, but briskly, and her shining blond hair had been pulled back into a neat chignon.

She turned and caught sight of him, then motioned for him to hurry up. "I thought you'd never get here!" Liesel exclaimed with a laugh. She handed him the reins for a tall black horse. "Here's your horse. His name is Ritter."

Then turning, she swiftly mounted Madchen, and sat, grinning down at him. Karl mounted Ritter, and they trotted out of the stable yard. As they reached the open meadow, Liesel urged Madchen into a gallop.

"Race you!" she called, laughing in sheer delight.

"What? Liesel!" Karl laughed, setting off after her.

Finally, they slowed as they crested the hill. Karl looked back at the manor house, which seemed small from this distance.

"I wish you could stay here," Liesel said, "And never have to go back to stuffy old Berlin."

"Oh, Liesel, you know I must," Karl said.

"We have such fun whenever you're here," Liesel said wistfully. "How long can you stay?"

"Only until tomorrow," Karl said.

Liesel's face fell. "Well, hurry back."

Karl smiled softly. "I'll always come back."

"I know," Liesel whispered.

Karl grinned. "Enough sad stuff! I'll be back for your birthday."

"You'd better!" Liesel exclaimed.

Karl squinted up at the sky. It was dark, and the air had grown cooler.

"It looks like it might rain," he said

"Race you back?" Liesel asked.

"You're on!" Karl replied, already racing forward. Liesel followed, leaning low over Madchen's neck.

As they approached the stables, the skies opened up, and rain fell in large droplets. Karl and Liesel slid down from their horses and walked briskly to the stable.

A groom took the saddle Liesel and handed her a thick cloth. She dried Madchen and led her to her stall, speaking softly to her the entire time. She rubbed Madchen's soft nose and then gave her a crisp apple.

Shutting the stall door, Liesel turned back to Karl, who stood waiting patiently with Ritter. "Come on, I'll show you his stall."

After putting Ritter in his stall, they paused at the stable door, watching the rain pour down in sheets.

"You ready?" Karl said, taking her hand.

Liesel nodded, and the pair ran out into the rain, dashing up the path to the manor house.

• • •

Herman found Klara in the library, pausing at the door for a moment to look at her as she read. "I've been summoned to Berlin," he said as he sat down next to her. "They've offered me a position in the government and asked for my help."

"Why, that's wonderful!" Klara exclaimed, putting aside her book. "What will be your duties?"

"I'll be a part of the Ministry of Economics," Herman said. "Ensuring that the factories around Berlin are operating at peak performance, increasing their efficiency, that sort of thing."

"I'm so happy for you!" Klara said, throwing her arms around his neck.

"I believe it will be a good position, and one that could lead to more," Herman agreed. "I leave for Berlin tomorrow morning."

"How long do you think you'll have to stay there?" Klara drew back.

"The letter mentioned several meetings, so I imagine around a week," he replied.

"I'll have the maids pack your things."

"Thank you, dear," he said. She stood and bent to kiss his cheek, then left the study, skirts swirling around her legs.

He watched her go, thinking of her clear blue eyes and shining blond hair. Truly, it was from Klara that Liesel had gotten her beauty, a beauty that she was unaware of, but that expressed itself to everyone she met. Klara too, had not lost any of the beauty and charm and energy that had drawn Herman to her nearly twenty years ago.

Herman looked down at the letter in his hands, pondering the contents once again. He sank into the chair Klara had vacated, letting his gaze rest on the rich, dark wood of the bookshelves lining the walls of the library. Next to their dark colour, the spines of the books leapt off the shelves with their bright colours and gold lettering.

The reality of just what he was leaving settled deep inside Herman. In the pit of his stomach, he wondered why the government had called him into service right now, with so many unknowns lurking before them. He felt a flicker of unease, but he disregarded it, instead running his fingers over the Ministry of Economics embossed letterhead.

The stirrings of pride overwhelmed the vague unease he felt, and Herman straightened his shoulders unconsciously.

They asked for my help.

Chapter Two

"Where are we going?" Karl said as he followed Liesel down the hall. "You'll see," Liesel replied. She led him around the house to a small staircase, hidden within a little-known passage off of a back hallway.

Karl squinted into the dark staircase. "I didn't even know this was here."

"It's not the staircase I wanted to show you, it's what's underneath," Liesel answered.

Liesel felt around underneath one of the ornate mouldings that followed the line of the stairs up. There was a faint click, and a panel clicked open. Liesel tugged at the panel, sliding it open the rest of the way.

"You'd never know it was here," Karl's eyes widened as he peered inside.

"Come on," Liesel beckoned him inside. She clicked on a flashlight, shining the beam into the dark passage ahead of them.

He followed her inside, waiting as she slid the panel shut, closing them inside. "Why'd you shut it?" he asked, looking at her face, lit by the glow of the flashlight.

"Because it's a secret, silly!" Liesel said with a laugh.

"No one else knows about this?"

"No one but my parents and me," Liesel replied. "Now come on!"

She walked along the passageway, further inside. It was dark, and just wide enough for the two to walk side by side. At six feet four, Karl's head nearly reached the ceiling of the passage, but Liesel could walk comfortably.

"Where does this go?" Karl asked.

"Just wait," Liesel said.

Above them, they could hear the creaks of the floor as people walked around upstairs, but aside from that, the passage was silent. Finally, they reached a dead end. Liesel pressed a small button and another panel clicked open. Karl gasped and Liesel smiled. They stepped from the passageway, blinking from the sudden light, into a small sitting room, used for receiving guests.

"That's incredible," Karl said. "We came all the way from the back of the house to the front through that tunnel!"

"Yes," Liesel said with a grin.

"When did you find it?" he asked, looking back towards the panel, where it blended perfectly with the wall around it.

"Several weeks ago, I think. We've owned the estate for years and years, but I've been doing some exploring recently. Father told me he found some of the tunnels when he was a boy, but I've found some other ones. This house is full of them."

"But why? Who put them here?"

Liesel shrugged. "Father said some of them were put in when the house was very first built, as a place for one of the old counts to hide things from prying eyes. Some of the tunnels were added during the Great War, in case of any trouble." She laughed. "I suppose some of my ancestors were paranoid." Liesel glanced out the window. "Oh look, it's stopped raining!"

"Would you like to go for a walk?" Karl said.

"Of course," she replied. "Just let me get a coat."

• • •

Later that night, Liesel lay in her bed, unable to sleep.

Their walk had been different. Different than the playful romps they so often had. Different than the morning's ride, always running, racing each other. Their walk had been slower, quieter, as they meandered over the von Schwarzkopf estate. Liesel shivered. She thought of the way he had taken her hand, sending little tingles up her arm. His eyes had softened as he looked at her, and she wondered what he thought when he looked into her eyes.

This was Karl. She had grown up with him. Gone to school in Berlin with him during the winter, spent summers racing across their neighbouring estates.

They had learned to ride the same summer, ridden all over their estates every summer after that. She had watched as he learned to shoot one summer, laughing at his misses and cheering when he hit the target. He had danced with her at her very first ball, making her laugh and easing her nerves. Together, they had watched the older men and women around them, mimicking their actions and laughing at their own mistakes.

Liesel smiled at the memories. He was her neighbour, her childhood playmate, her best friend. And now, he had taken her hand, and all of a sudden he was something more. Butterflies flitted in her stomach as she considered these new feelings, making her feel more grown up, and yet child-like, unknowing.

She shook her head, putting those thoughts away. For now, at least.

• • •

In the guest room, Karl rolled over in bed, opening his eyes. It was dark, and although the bed was comfortable, he could not sleep.

Liesel's face, with those laughing blue eyes, floated before his eyes. How different she could be. This morning's headlong rush, her eyes always gleaming, daring him to beat her. And then, this afternoon's walk. How delicately pretty she seemed, with her eyes soft as she looked at him. Her hair, shining blond as it blew lightly in the breeze.

He shut his eyes firmly, and rolled over once again, trying to put the matter out of his mind.

• • •

The next morning dawned dark and gloomy. Rain fell in sheets against the windows, and thick clouds obscured any view of the sun.

At breakfast, talk focused on Herman's new position, then turned to Liesel's upcoming birthday.

"I certainly hope it isn't like this on the day of the ball," Liesel said, glancing out the French doors.

"I'm sure it won't be," Klara said, touching Liesel's shoulder. "And even so, the party will be in the ballroom."

"Yes, I suppose," Liesel consented. "But I do hope it's sunny."

Herman chuckled, shaking his head.

Finally, it was time for Herman and Karl to leave.

"Goodbye, Father," Liesel said, hugging him tightly.

Beside them, Karl kissed Klara on the cheek.

"Come again soon," she said.

Liesel stood back, as her mother said goodbye to her father, and Karl wrapped her up in a hug.

"Goodbye, Liesel," Karl said quietly. "I'll see you in August."

"I'll miss you," Liesel replied. "But I know you'll be back."

He gave a jaunty wave as he jogged out the door, pulling his coat collar tight against the rain, Herman following closely behind. Klara and Liesel watched as they got into their cars and drove down the long road, away, towards Berlin.

It rained the rest of that day, and Liesel roamed restlessly through the big house. She paced, glancing out of the windows occasionally, until at last, bedtime came, and she could go to her room.

Chapter Three

Days passed slowly at the von Schwarzkopf estate. Liesel often took to her mare, racing wildly, recklessly, across the meadows to escape the stifling heat that had settled upon them like a weight.

August came, and with it, her father. However, he could only stay for several days before having to return to Berlin.

The day before he left, he and Liesel rode out, up to a hill that rose up and allowed a view of the manor house below.

"I'm sorry I must leave again so soon," Herman said.

Liesel was silent for a moment, looking out at the lands before her. "I love Germany," she said finally, turning her blue eyes towards him.

Herman looked at her, his head cocked in confusion.

"Our country needs you," Liesel continued softly, and comprehension dawned on Herman's face.

"Thank you," he said quietly.

"And it's not as if you'll be gone forever!" she laughed. Her eyes gleamed. "Race you back!"

They took off, thundering across the grass, young once again, if only for this brief ride. Too soon, they would return to reality: Herman to Berlin and Liesel to the adulthood that loomed before her. But for now, they laughed as only two who were as closely connected as this pair could.

The next day, she waved goodbye as his black car disappeared down the long road once again and then turned back to the house to help her mother with preparations for her birthday.

The date was coming quickly and there was still so much to do—food, drink, and music all had to be organized. Together, Klara and Liesel had created the menu and given it to the cook. Wine arrived from Berlin, and Klara had arranged for musicians from Berlin to come out to the estate for the evening of the ball.

Liesel could hardly wait to see their house filled with guests, overflowing with music and laughter. There would be dancing, and friends... and Karl.

• • •

"Liesel," Klara called excitedly from the front hall.

"What is it, Mother?" Liesel replied, poking out her head from the front sitting room, where she had been reading a letter from one of her school friends.

"Your dress!" Klara exclaimed. "It's here! The maids took it to your room!"

"Really?" Liesel cried. She dashed towards her bedroom.

Several weeks earlier, they'd gone to a dress shop in Berlin and ordered the dress that awaited them. Now, Klara buttoned up the tiny loops that clasped the entire back of the dress together, and stepped back, turning Liesel to face a large mirror.

Liesel turned, and drew in a breath at her reflection. The dress was a deep, cobalt blue that drew out the colour in her eyes. The silhouette was slim, hugging her figure and accenting her height. From the waist down, the skirt became full, sweeping the floor, yet flying out in layers upon layers as she spun like a little girl in her first dress. With the dress, they had ordered a pair of sleek, elbow-length gloves that perfectly matched the blue of the dress, and Liesel drew these on now. Klara did up the ten small buttons that sparkled like sapphires on each glove, then stepped back, taking in her daughter's appearance.

"You're beautiful," she said softly.

"Oh, Mother!" was all Liesel could say. Her eyes shone as she looked at Klara.

Klara brushed her thumb over the fabric of Liesel's gloves and then sighed. "We should put it away now, until the ball."

"I suppose you're right," Liesel agreed.

Carefully they removed the dress, laying it back in its protective wrappings. Liesel cast one wistful glance back before leaving her room and returning to her letter.

Chapter Four

Two weeks later, unable to sleep, Liesel crept downstairs. The moon shone brightly through the windows, lighting the darkened house.

Reaching a set of large double doors, she opened one a crack and slipped through. She stood in the von Schwarzkopf ballroom. It was a large room, its floors cleaned and polished in preparation for dancing. Paintings hung on the walls, and a large set of French doors at the opposite end opened onto a large terrace with a view of the surrounding countryside.

Liesel shivered with excitement. Tomorrow night, she would step into this ballroom and join a host of Berlin's, of Germany's, most distinguished citizens.

Taking a step forward, she curtsied, her movements echoing in the empty ballroom. Raising her arm to an imaginary partner, she moved lightly around the room, stopping as she reached the French doors. She leaned against them and lifted her face to the moon that shone so brightly above.

A moment later, she yawned, breaking the spell, and tip-toed back to her room.

The next day, maids bustled through the big house, finishing the final preparations for that night's ball. The musicians arrived, and the servants carried platters of food and decanters of wine to the ballroom.

Upstairs, alone in her room, Liesel heard the voices of guests beginning to arrive. As she gazed at her reflection in the mirror, Klara entered, holding a small case.

"Open it," she said, passing it to Liesel.

Carefully, Liesel lifted the lid and found a necklace of sparkling sapphires. "It's beautiful," she murmured.

"It's yours," Klara replied with a smile. "Let me put it on."

Gently, Klara drew the necklace around Liesel's neck and clasped it. Then dropping a kiss on Liesel's hair, she held out a hand. "Ready?"

"Yes," Liesel said, squaring her shoulders.

Side by side, they descended the stairs. Klara slowed at the ballroom doors, allowing Liesel to enter first.

"I love you," she whispered, so quietly that Liesel did not even glance back.

Heads turned as Liesel entered the room, and for a split second, her nerves overcame her, and she briefly pondered the idea of running away. Instead, she took a deep breath and smiled.

Liesel soon found herself laughing and talking with a crowd of young people she knew from the many parties and events she'd attended growing up.

Suddenly, Liesel looked up to see Karl's piercing green eyes on her. He stood a short distance away, champagne glass in hand, quietly watching her.

"Will you excuse me?" Liesel said, walking towards Karl. "I'm so glad you came!"

"I told you I would," he replied softly, looking deep into her eyes.

"Karl!" a feminine voice interrupted. "You simply must come dance with me!"

At that moment, a young woman came into view. Short, but slim, Brigitta Maartens tossed her sleek brown hair as she spoke.

"Brigitta," Liesel said stiffly. "I'm so glad you were able to come."

Brigitta's smile never reached her eyes. "And I'm sure you won't mind if I have a dance with Karl," she said.

"Certainly not," Liesel replied. "I can't neglect my other guests." She turned away, not wanting to watch the pair whirl away in each other's arms.

All of a sudden, a quiet voice startled her.

"May I have this dance?"

It was Herman. He held out his hand to her.

"Certainly, sir," Liesel replied with mock formality, smiling happily. She placed her hand in his, and he led her to the dance floor.

"Are you enjoying yourself?" Herman asked.

"Oh yes!" Liesel replied, her eyes shining.

They spun around, listening to the music and the conversations that swirled around them. Then, a young man wearing a uniform of the army of the Third Reich approached.

"May I have this dance?" he asked politely.

Herman nodded, releasing Liesel from his arms.

For the next hour, Liesel found herself being swept across the ballroom floor by a multitude of young men. Some paid her extravagant compliments that made her blush. Some joked and teased until she had to laugh. And some were content to be silent and simply lead her in the dance. Finally, Liesel was able to stop and catch her breath. She sipped slowly from a glass of champagne, watching the dancers before her.

Directly in front of her, Herman and Klara danced gracefully, Klara wrapped comfortably in Herman's arms. He leaned down and whispered in her ear, and she smiled.

The music changed, becoming slower, softer.

"May I have this dance?" Karl asked from behind her shoulder.

"Of course," Liesel replied. Setting aside her champagne glass, she took his hand.

"You look lovely," he said, as they began to dance.

They moved lightly across the room, slowing as they neared the doors to the terrace. With a glance towards one another, and a single look over their shoulders, they slipped through the doors, unnoticed, onto the terrace.

"It's so much cooler out here," Liesel said, grateful for the light breeze that blew across her face.

Strains of music sounded faintly through the closed doors, and Karl held out his hand again. Liesel giggled and they began to dance across the terrace. Karl spun her, and her skirts unfurled like waves in the clear blue sea.

At that moment, it seemed as though the world had shrunk to just the two of them. She slowed, smiling up at him, and they leaned against the railing. For an instant, Liesel felt the brush of Karl's lips on her cheek, and she looked towards him, but he had already turned away. As she gazed at his face in the moonlight, she basked in the feeling of contentment that swept over her.

They stood looking out at the stars, their futures, it seemed on this perfect night, so bright ahead of them.

Chapter Five

September 3, 1939

The news came by telegram, delivered to the von Schwarzkopf estate. Liesel was in the library, gazing dreamily out the window at the trees that had begun to turn from green to gold, signalling the end of summer.

All of a sudden, she heard an exclamation, then the sound of muffled crying. Dashing out of the room, she halted in surprise. Klara stood stock still in the middle of the hall, holding a sheet of paper limply in one hand.

"Mother, what is it?" Liesel asked worriedly, hastening towards her. "What's wrong?"

Without a word, Klara handed the paper to Liesel.

"*Germany at war STOP Must remain in Berlin longer than planned STOP Don't worry STOP Love you both STOP.*"

"At war?" she said stupidly. "How can we be at war?"

Klara enveloped Liesel in a hug, and they held each other in silence. Liesel felt her eyes brim with tears, and she struggled to keep them from falling.

"Don't worry, Mother," Liesel said finally. "I'm sure it will be over quickly. And besides, Father will be safe in Berlin."

"I suppose you're right," Klara agreed, wiping her eyes and smiling weakly. "But I can't help..." her voice trailed off.

"Mother, Father wouldn't want you to worry," Liesel reminded her. "He's not in any danger." But her words were empty promises, hollow.

Liesel saddled Madchen that afternoon and galloped out of the stable yard, across the meadows, to the hill she and Herman had sat on top of, those long days ago. How different things were now, Liesel thought, gazing down at the manor house.

"Before, I feared nothing," Liesel murmured to herself. "And now... Father is safe, but Karl..." her voice trailed off, and the tears she had refused to let fall, fell now.

"Karl could go at any moment," she whispered, and it was now that the deadly realization of war settled on her, like a shackle she couldn't escape. As if the grim shadow of death hovered behind her, waiting to strike.

Days passed. Karl sent a telegram, reassuring them that he would be remaining in Berlin with his SS unit for the foreseeable future, and Liesel allowed herself to breathe a sigh of relief.

She could hardly believe that only three weeks ago, she and Karl had stood just like this, gazing out from the terrace. Now, thousands of German men were fighting in Poland, and summer's relaxing days had come to an end.

• • •

As September faded into October, Klara and Liesel prepared for the move back to their winter home in Berlin. Though several servants would remain at the estate to care for the horses and keep the grounds, the majority of servants would be returning to Berlin with them and, for days, the house was filled with the sounds of cleaning and packing. The war seemed far away, distant.

The first few snowflakes of the year drifted down from the sky as the family prepared to drive to Berlin. In the stables, Liesel stroked Madchen's copper neck, murmuring goodbye to her. Then stepping outside, she glanced one more time towards the large house and climbed into the waiting car, where Herman and Klara sat patiently.

"Ready to go?" Herman asked.

"Yes," Liesel and Klara replied in unison, and the car pulled away.

Liesel looked back, once, as they rounded the bend, and then faced resolutely forward for the remainder of the trip.

Later that night, Liesel stood alone in her darkened bedroom in the Berlin house, gazing at the city from the second-storey window. Trunks filled with yet unpacked clothes cast shadows on the walls. The sky above was dark, the moon obscured by clouds, and snowflakes drifted down lazily. With a sigh, Liesel turned away, crawling into bed. As she listened to the buzz of traffic, she missed the estate, with its peace and quiet.

Summer seemed miles away.

Chapter Six

June 1940

Winter's long, dismal days had passed. The skies were blue once more, and the German army, after several months of inaction, had mounted a series of successful campaigns in France. The resulting victories had left the city, the country, in a jubilant mood as summer arrived.

With the return of spring, the von Schwarzkopf family moved back out to the estate, though Herman stayed behind because of his increasing responsibilities. Even so, Liesel was glad to be returning to the estate's wide-open spaces.

Liesel sighed with contentment as she gazed out the window. Karl had managed to get away from Berlin, and would be arriving soon, with plans to stay for a week.

When she saw his car pull up to the house, Liesel hurried outside, shielding her eyes from the sun. He stepped out of the car, backlit by the sun, and for a moment, Liesel couldn't see him.

But soon he was slinging his arms around her shoulders and pulling her close.

"Good to see you, Liesel," he said, as he rested his cheek against her hair.

"I'm so glad you're here," Liesel replied.

All of a sudden, she raised her head, her eyes glinting. "Do you want to ride?" she asked.

"Of course," Karl replied.

"Race you to the stables!" Liesel cried. She took off, laughing as he snagged her wrist, stopping her from running.

"Can't win now, can you?" Karl teased.

Liesel made a face and together they ran to the stables.

• • •

That evening, they strolled lazily beyond the house, arm in arm. Karl couldn't believe the change in Liesel. It had been so long since he'd seen her, it seemed as though she'd changed from a girl into a woman in a split second.

Stopping for a moment, they gazed towards Berlin. Dusk was falling, and the city lights sparkled in the distance. Karl watched Liesel as she looked towards the city, her face fixed in a smile of blissful oblivion. His own face grew hooded as he thought about the war. Although Liesel softened him, brought his smile back to his eyes, that smile soon disappeared when he returned to Berlin.

Thoughts of war turned him into stone, into a cold, unfeeling man, one who Liesel would hardly recognize. He never let that world intrude into the carefree existence they had together. He would never show Liesel the man he was in Berlin.

Karl turned back to look at her, relishing the feel of her hand on his arm. She was looking away from him, and he observed the curve of her neck, looking at her hair as it caught the last glimmers of fading light.

Here, the trials of war faded away. When he was with her, he could almost believe he still shared her innocence.

• • •

Herman surprised them with a visit the next morning. Upon seeing him, Klara leapt from the table and ran to him.

"You didn't tell me you were coming home," she said as she threw her arms around him.

When they returned to the table, Herman swept Liesel up in a hug. "Liesel, is it possible you've grown?"

"Oh, Father," Liesel replied with a laugh.

"I managed to get away from Berlin for a day or two. It's been too long since I saw you both."

The rest of the week passed in a haze of laughter and pleasant company. Karl and Liesel rode and walked and explored the grounds of the estate, enjoying the time in each other's company.

The last night of Karl's visit, they stood together on the terrace in comfortable silence. Liesel's thoughts drifted back to August, one year before. In her mind's eye, she still felt the rustle of her dress as they danced, his lips on her cheek, and the contentment she had felt as they stood gazing out at the stars. Now, here they stood, older now, but as if nothing had changed between them.

• • •

Two months later, Liesel was jolted awake by distant thunder. She jumped out of bed and looked out the window. In the distance, flashes of light lit up the night sky as explosions sounded. Berlin was under fire.

"What?" she murmured in confusion. "What's going on?"

Klara burst into her room. "Liesel, are you all right?"

"Yes, but Father..." Liesel said, eyes fixed on the explosions in the distance.

"We'll have to wait until morning to find out," Klara replied shakily, taking Liesel's hand.

"I won't be able to sleep," she said.

"I know," Klara whispered.

They sat together the rest of that long night, until finally, dawn came.

Later that day, a telegram arrived from Herman.

"*Am safe STOP Very little damage to city STOP None killed STOP Don't worry STOP*," Klara read out loud, relaxing for the first time since the explosions had sounded.

Throughout the next month, Herman slowly sent news to the estate through newspapers and letters. Germany's retaliation had been swift. British cities were soon being targeted by German planes, rather than the original goal of British airfields. The Berlin *National Observer* proclaimed, "Berlin targeted by British bombers! Luftwaffe to retaliate!"

"How dare they!" Liesel exclaimed. "These are our people, not soldiers! They're innocent! Why would they do this to us?"

As Herman had reported, however, Berlin had suffered very little damage, and, as September faded into October, Klara and Liesel returned to Berlin for the winter.

• • •

Christmas came with a break of parties and fun. Though nothing would be grand due to rationing, most seized the opportunity to put the war aside, if only for a brief time.

It was several days before Christmas, and Karl and Liesel were driving back to the von Schwarzkopf's home from an evening out. Snow lay on the ground and stars twinkled in the black velvet sky above.

Liesel looked out the car window and realized she didn't recognize the way. "Where are we going?" she asked.

"You'll see," Karl replied.

"Karl!"

"You'll see," he repeated, grinning at her as she fidgeted in the passenger seat.

Finally, Karl stopped the car at a park. Opening their doors, they stepped out onto the snowy ground. Liesel gasped with delight. Trees surrounded them, delicate hoarfrost coating each branch.

"Would you like to go for a walk?" Karl asked.

Liesel nodded, taking hold of his arm. They walked slowly through the park, Liesel gazing all around with wonder.

Finally, Karl spoke.

"I was wondering if," he began, and Liesel waited patiently. "...if I could call on you."

"Of course," Liesel replied, wrinkling her nose.

Karl rubbed the back of his neck. "I mean, as more than a friend."

Liesel's face broke into a smile as she realized what he was asking. "I'd like that," she said.

Karl grinned and pulled her to him, bending down to kiss her cheek. They stood together for long minutes, until Liesel shivered in the frosty air.

"I'd better get you home," Karl said reluctantly.

Hand in hand, they returned to the car and pulled away from that magical place; a winter white fairyland.

That Christmas, presents were few, and the meal was simple, but Liesel's heart overflowed with happiness. Karl visited often over the holidays, and he and Liesel walked and talked and laughed, enjoying each other's company. In those moments, the war seemed nonexistent.

• • •

In April, the war became a deadly reality for Liesel. Karl was being sent to Greece with his SS unit.

"When do you leave?" Liesel asked as they sat alone in the sitting room in the von Schwarzkopf home.

"Greece is expected to surrender at any moment, so we'll be leaving next week," Karl told her. "Don't cry," he begged, seeing the tears glistening in her clear blue eyes. "I'm sure it will be short, and there's really no danger."

Liesel nodded, not trusting herself to speak.

"I'll be fine," Karl repeated, taking her hand. "And we'll write."

"Promise?" Liesel said.

"I promise."

The week passed far too quickly for Liesel, and soon they stood at the train station. Herman shook Karl's hand, wishing him luck, and Klara gave him a hug.

"Come back soon," she said.

Karl's mother, Maria, hugged him tightly, and his father, Friedrich, gave him a firm handshake.

"Good luck, Son," he said gruffly.

Liesel stood watching, biting her lip, trying not to cry. Finally, Karl stood in front of her, lifting her hands and clasping them gently.

"I'll miss you," he said softly, pulling her to him.

She buried her face in his uniform, letting her tears fall on the grey cloth. He held her tightly for a moment, then pulled away.

"I have to go," he whispered, dipping down to kiss her.

"Goodbye, Karl," Liesel whispered.

"Goodbye, Liesel." Karl brushed his fingers lightly against her cheek and then he was gone, shouldering his knapsack and climbing aboard the train.

Liesel watched the train pull away, catching a glimpse of his blond head as he leaned out to wave.

As they drove home, a light rain fell, splattering on the windshield of the car. The next day, April 20, 1941, the newspapers proclaimed Germany's victory and Greece's surrender. Liesel celebrated, yet her heart still feared for Karl. Where was he, she wondered. Was he in Greece yet? Or still on the train?

Chapter Seven

Two weeks later, Karl received a letter. A faint scent, the scent of a summer day, of flowers and wind and bright blue sky, still lingered on the envelope. Liesel's scent. Karl breathed deeply and then slit the envelope, unfolding the letter inside.

> *"Dear, Karl,*
>
> *I miss you so much. I'm sure you're in Greece by now, and I hope everything is going well. We got the news of Greece's surrender the day after you left.*
>
> *The sky is so blue here, Karl. Is it blue where you are right now? I hope it is.*
>
> *Time is passing slowly. I cannot wait for your return. Berlin has stayed much the same since you left. The only news is that Brigitta has gotten engaged! His name is Kurt. He is in the army, so they plan to get married as soon as the war ends. It is to be 'a grand wedding' as she explained to me.*
>
> *Oh, Karl, I wish the war was over! I wish we could go back to the way things were. I wish you could come home.*
>
> *I must go now, but I love you, Karl.*
>
> *Yours, Liesel."*

Karl closed his eyes, picturing her face, with her blue eyes and blond hair, smiling up at him.

"Dear, Liesel,

I miss you too. The sky here is blue. Blue like your eyes, and I think of you when I see it. I wish I could see you, but I'm sure I'll be home soon. Please don't worry about me. I'm sure Brigitta is very happy. She always did like things like that.

I miss you so much, today especially. I close my eyes and I picture your face. It feels like forever since I've seen you.

I love you, Liesel.

Yours, Karl."

Over the next weeks, Liesel marked time by letters, coming and going.

"Dear, Karl,

Perhaps you know this news already, but if not, here it is. We've invaded Russia. I confess, I know nothing about the campaign, as everyone calls it, but it's the most exciting news I have to tell you.

Summer is passing, and I haven't seen you in so long. Remember all the fun we used to have at the estate? Riding and walking and talking. And remember my birthday ball? We danced on the terrace and looked out at the stars. How long ago all that seems. I can hardly believe it.

What is Greece like? I want to hear all about it.

I can't wait for the war to end. Then perhaps we could go to Greece. Or anywhere. I would go anywhere with you, Karl.

Love, Liesel."

Karl folded the letter and pocketed it once again. Around him, the evidence of war was unmistakable. The people of Greece fought hunger and poverty. Their eyes told of their empty stomachs, while their thin frames proclaimed the fact to all who looked. This was completely foreign to the luxurious life Liesel enjoyed in Berlin. He decided he would never tell her.

"Dear, Liesel,
Greece can be rather pretty at times, although not half as pretty as you. Someday, perhaps after the war, I shall take you to Greece. But not now, darling.
I hope you have been keeping busy, enjoying the summer. When I get back, promise me you will take me riding. It has been so long.
Keep writing, Liesel. I love to hear from you.
Missing you so much, Karl."

"Dear, Karl,
This war is wretched! I can scarcely believe I will be twenty in one month, and it is still continuing. It's been two years! When will it end? I just want things to go back to the way they used to be!
I wish you were home.
Love, Liesel.
P.S. I promise we'll go riding, so hurry home!"

"Dear, Liesel,
I hope I will be home for your birthday, but if not, I apologize now. I wish I could be with you.
The heat is stifling here. Thankfully, there are breezes from the sea, but right now, riding with you at the estate sounds much more pleasant.
I'm sorry my letters have been short. I don't have much spare time here.
I love you.
Karl."

Liesel refolded the letter and tucked it away in a small carved box that contained every letter she had received from Karl. She re-read them often, savouring the words, yet wishing he were here to say them in person.

That evening, Liesel picked at her food listlessly.

"Liesel dear, are you feeling all right?" Klara asked.

"Hmm?" Liesel said absently, looking up from her plate.

"I asked if you were feeling all right."

"I'm fine," Liesel said.

Herman frowned. "What's wrong, Liesel?"

"You can tell us," Klara said.

Liesel's shoulders slumped. "I miss Karl."

"Oh, I know, dear," Klara said softly.

"I wish he could come home. He's been gone for three months!" Liesel lifted her hands helplessly, then let them fall back into her lap.

"He will be back, Liesel. You just have to be patient," Klara reminded her.

"I know," Liesel murmured. "He writes, but he hardly tells me anything about what he's doing!"

Herman sighed, and when he spoke, his words were heavy. "This is war, Liesel. Do you really *want* to know everything that he's doing?"

"I do!" Liesel insisted. "Because I want to know about him!"

Herman shook his head. "He's trying to protect you, Liesel. From the war. From the fighting and killing. From the harsh realities he sees every day."

"I am not a child!" Liesel clenched her fist. "I don't need protecting!"

"You don't," Klara said, laying her hand over Liesel's fist and gently loosening her fingers. "But I believe, Liesel, that Karl is doing the right thing by not telling you all he does. Do you want to feel that burden?"

"I suppose not," Liesel admitted grudgingly.

Klara squeezed Liesel's shoulder. "But I also know that Karl wouldn't want to see you like this. He wouldn't want you to worry. He'll be fine, I'm sure."

"I suppose," Liesel agreed slowly. Picking up her fork, she began to eat, and Klara's worried face relaxed.

August 9, 1941

"Dear, Karl,

There was a bombing raid last night. Thankfully, not much was damaged. And we are safe here at the estate. It's a little frightening though, to see the flashes and hear the explosions during the night.

I hope you're safe. I worry about you. And I'm missing you.
Love, Liesel."

"Dear, Liesel,
I'm so glad to hear you're safe. I wish I could be there! I'm sure
I'll be home before winter though. I'm sorry that I won't be back
before your birthday... so happy twentieth!
I can't wait until I'm home and we can be together again. It's
been a long time, but for now, we must make the best of it.
Missing you, Karl."

"Dear, Karl,
My birthday has come and gone. I can't say I feel any different
now that I'm twenty.
Mother and I are going to stay at the estate this fall, and likely
the winter as well. Father thinks it will be safer for us, and I'm
happy with his decision.
Hurry home!
Love, Liesel."

"Dear, Liesel,
Your father is a wise man. I'm glad that you (and Klara) will
be safe if Berlin is bombed again. We've received news that we will
be arriving in Berlin on September 12. See you soon!
I love you, Liesel.
Yours, Karl."

"Mother! Mother!" Liesel shouted.

"What is it?" Klara called. "What's wrong?"

Liesel ran down the staircase, fairly floating, and waved a piece of paper in front of Klara's eyes.

"Karl's coming home!" Liesel sang out.

Klara snatched the letter from Liesel's waving hand. "September 12! That's only two days away! How wonderful!" She took in Liesel's sparkling blue eyes and flushed cheeks. "I take it someone's happy?" she teased.

"Only a little," Liesel said with a laugh.

"I'm so glad," Klara said, reaching out to give her a hug.

"So, we'll go to the train station?" Liesel asked, her brow furrowing.

"Of course," Klara replied, and Liesel danced away, her grin never leaving her face.

A few moments later, Klara heard Liesel's shout of happiness as she galloped away from the house, and smiled at her daughter's enthusiasm.

Two days later, Liesel stood at the train station, waiting anxiously.

Friedrich and Maria, and Herman and Klara, all stood behind her as the train made its way into the station. There was a burst of noise and excited chatter as the men began to disembark from the train. Liesel stood on tip-toe, searching for Karl. Finally, she spotted his tall figure moving through the crowd, and she waved excitedly.

"Karl!"

At the sound of his name, Karl looked up, scanning the crowd, and saw her. He grinned and hurried towards her. Pushing against the crowd, Liesel made her way to meet him, breaking into a run. Karl dropped his knapsack, picked her up in his arms, and swung her around until she laughed with delight.

"I missed you so much," she exclaimed, half sobbing, half smiling.

"Don't cry," he begged. "I'm home!"

He set her down, keeping his arms around her waist. She laid her head on his chest, feeling the steady heartbeat within.

"Your letters smell like you," he said. Liesel raised her head to look up at him. "Like summer," he clarified. "I've missed you."

They stood like that for a long moment, until their parents hurried up to them. Reluctantly, Liesel let go and stepped back as a flurry of hugs and handshakes began. She watched him embrace his mother, memorizing his face, his eyes, his smile.

He glanced up and met her gaze. "I love you," he mouthed to her over Maria's head.

Finally, they returned to their cars, Liesel and Karl walking hand in hand.

"I'm sorry I missed your birthday," he said.

"That's all right. It's enough that you're home," Liesel replied.

As she gazed into his eyes, however, a flicker of uneasiness came over her. His eyes, such a deep green, seemed cold, hard, different than before. He had changed during the summer. Liesel shivered. The feeling of unease was soon gone, however, and Liesel pushed the thoughts away, forgetting about them.

Chapter Eight

On their last day in Berlin, Liesel walked past the drawing room where Herman and Klara sat, talking earnestly.

"...could not believe it... dreadful... can't imagine why..." Herman's voice trickled out to Liesel in the hall.

"...not serious... surely not..." Liesel could barely make out Klara's soft response.

"...hardly believe... myself..."

Liesel tapped on the door, and both Herman and Klara looked up.

"What is it, Liesel?" Herman asked.

"Karl and I are going out for a walk," Liesel said.

"Have fun, dear," Klara replied with a smile.

Liesel waved and hurried to the front door, where Karl was waiting, pushing away all thoughts of her parents' conversation.

In the sitting room, Herman watched her go, a frown creasing his forehead. "What do you think she'll say?"

Klara shook her head. "I don't know. I hope she'll see why we have to do this. I believe she has a tender heart, enough to take a risk in order to care for others."

Herman studied Klara intently. "What about you?"

Klara closed her eyes. "I'd be lying if I said I wasn't scared." She opened her eyes. "But I believe this is the right thing to do."

"We can back away from this," Herman said softly. "If you think the risk is too great."

"No," Klara said firmly. "No, we can't. This is the right thing to do. I know it, even if I am scared."

Herman looked away from her. "I hope it is."

Klara laid her hand on his. "It is," she said evenly. "You knew it, when you saw those people. I knew it, when you told me about them. Some risks are worth taking, Herman."

"I know," he said heavily. "But I hate to put you in danger." He groaned, low and distressed. "I just... I couldn't leave this alone, Klara. It's been haunting my thoughts. The sight of all those people, hurting, starving, broken." He looked at her, his brown eyes anguished. "How can they do this? This isn't how Jesus would want us to act. This isn't how he would want us to treat people. I can't believe that, no matter what my government tells me. They want us all to believe what they tell us, that the Jews are worthless, but I can't believe it! I know it's not true." He looked around the room, taking in the fine furnishings, the luxury all around him. "I can't face Jesus when I die, knowing I could have helped people and didn't."

Klara squeezed his hand. "Some risks are worth taking, Herman." She paused, and a glimmer of a smile appeared on her lips as she looked at him. "We'll be all right."

The next day, Liesel and Klara returned to the estate. The trees were adorned with fall colours of red, yellow, and gold, and Liesel sighed as she looked out at them. Winter would soon be upon them, but with none of the fun of past winters. Because of the war, social events were non-existent, and Liesel could already feel the coming snows trapping her within the estate.

About a week later, Herman arrived at the estate. He found Liesel outside and said a quick hello before hurrying to the front door. "Where's your mother?" he asked.

"In the sitting room," Liesel replied.

"Thank you," Herman called. Liesel watched him go, frowning. She had never seen Herman so preoccupied.

Later that day, she watched with confusion as he sped away, back to Berlin. Over the next two days, Herman came and went, only staying long enough to talk to Klara before leaving again.

He was back again, and Liesel could hear him taking to her mother in the drawing room. Narrowing her eyes, she grabbed a flashlight and sneaked towards the staircase at the back of the house. She pressed a small button and slipped the panel open, pulling it shut behind her.

She hurried through the dark passageway, keeping the flashlight beam trained towards the floor in order to keep from tripping. When she reached the end of the passage, she pressed another small button, and a peephole opened. Liesel pressed her eye to it, catching a glimpse of Herman and Klara. They sat close together, murmuring to each other, so quietly that Liesel could only make out the occasional word.

"...papers..." Herman was saying.

"...safe... the passage... how long..." Klara asked.

"...dangerous... too long..." Herman replied.

All of a sudden, a noise sounded in the hall, and both Herman and Klara looked up quickly.

"...should go," Herman said.

"...when... tell her?" Klara replied.

"...wait... to see reason... I hope..." Herman said. "If not..."

Klara looked at him, solemn and silent. Then, getting to their feet, the two of them left the room. Liesel clicked the peephole shut, then sat down, leaning against the wall.

"What's going on?" she whispered. "Who were they talking about?"

She sat in the darkness, pondering this for long moments, until finally, she stood, and walked back down the long, dark passage.

• • •

Karl visited in October.

"I can only stay for two days," he warned Liesel.

"It's better than nothing!" Liesel replied happily.

That evening, they rode out into the meadows, escaping the manor house.

"My father's been acting a little strange lately," Liesel said as they came to a stop to let the horse rest.

"Strange?"

"He just seems preoccupied lately," Liesel said.

"I'm sure it's just because of his work in Berlin," Karl said, reaching over to brush his hand along her arm. "It has been keeping him busy."

"I suppose," Liesel agreed. "That's probably it."

As the sun set and shadows fell long across the ground, Karl and Liesel meandered back to the house. The next day, Karl drove away, Liesel waving to him from the front door.

• • •

The first snowflakes were falling, and November was on its way, when Herman returned to the estate once again.

That night, he and Klara called Liesel to their bedroom. The lights were dim, and they sat close together on the low couch beneath one of the bedroom windows. A fire crackled in the big stone fireplace, relieving the chill in the room. It was cozy, and Liesel was transported back to many happy childhood evenings spent listening to her parents read to her on that very couch.

A smile touched her lips briefly at the thought, and then she remembered her parents request for her to come.

"What is it, Father? Mother?" Liesel said, brows furrowed.

Klara glanced towards Herman, and he gave her a subtle nod.

"Your father and I have something very important to tell you," Klara said quietly. "Recently, your father was given a tour of a camp."

"A camp?"

"A camp where the German government is holding Jews. They go there to work and be contained. And be killed," Herman shifted in his seat, reaching out to take hold of Klara's hand.

"Killed?" Liesel wrinkled her brow. "Surely not."

"Yes," Herman replied. "And it's not the only one. There are dozens of them all across Germany."

"Why are you telling me this?" Liesel asked. "What does this have to do with us? With me?"

"Your mother and I have decided to help these people," Herman explained.

"They can hide at the estate on their way to Switzerland," Klara made a calming motion with her hand. "That's where many of them try to go."

Liesel stared at her parents, her eyes wide in disbelief.

"There *is* danger," Herman said seriously. "You cannot tell anyone."

"Not even Karl," Klara added. "No one but the three of us can know."

"What!" Liesel shrieked. "How could you do this?"

"Hush!" Herman said quickly.

"Liesel, these are people being killed, every day," Klara laid a hand on Liesel's knee. "That's wrong. You know that."

"Yes, Mother, I know," Liesel replied.

"They'll stay in some of the hidden passages for a short time before they continue on to Switzerland," Herman explained.

"Our job," Klara interjected, "is to keep them safe while they're here, and provide them anything we can to help them on their journey."

"What if we're found out?" Liesel leapt to her feet, gesturing wildly. "Then we'll be the ones who are killed, never mind them!"

"We have to take that chance," Herman said solemnly.

"I can't believe you're going to do this!" Liesel said angrily, looking back and forth between them. "I can't believe you would put us in danger like this! How could you! Our lives will be ruined!"

Klara looked worriedly at Herman.

"Liesel, you can't tell anyone about this," he said.

"Why would I?" Liesel scoffed. "It would destroy my life!"

"Our first group will be here before the first of December," Herman said. "It's our job to be sure the passages are ready before then."

"I'm sorry, Liesel," Klara said softly. "But we have to do what we know is right."

"Right! Is it right to put your daughter in danger like this? Is that right?" She whirled and stormed out of the room.

"Liesel," Herman called after her.

Klara laid a hand on his arm. "I'll go to her," she said.

She found Liesel standing at the window in her bedroom, gazing out into the dark night. The lights of Berlin twinkled in the distance.

Liesel stiffened as Klara placed a hand on her shoulder. They stood in silence for long moments.

"I wish you wouldn't do it," Liesel said finally, breaking the silence.

"Liesel, we..."

"I know it's wrong for them to be killed, but I don't want to be killed either!" Liesel's voice broke.

Klara pulled Liesel to her, hugging her tightly.

"I'm scared." Liesel whispered.

"I know," Klara murmured.

"Why do you have to do this?"

"Because it's right," Klara rubbed her hand up and down Liesel's back.

"I wish you wouldn't," Liesel said. "I don't want to live in fear! I don't want my life to change."

"Liesel, your life will always be changing," Klara said. "That *is* life."

"I know you have to do what you believe is right," Liesel said. "But I want to be safe. I don't want to be afraid."

"I know," Klara replied, releasing Liesel. "Go to sleep now, it's late." She kissed Liesel on the cheek and then left the room.

"I love you," she said as she shut the bedroom door.

• • •

"How is she?" Herman asked when Klara returned to their room.

"She's scared," Klara replied wearily. "Scared and angry."

"Angry?"

"Yes, angry," Klara said. "Angry at us for putting her in danger, and angry at her own fear."

Herman blew out a long breath. "I didn't know she would take it like this."

Klara came to sit on his knee, leaning her head on his shoulder. He put his arms around her, staring blankly at the wall.

"I'm sure she'll come around," Klara said softly. "And I know we made the right decision."

Herman turned to look at her. "I love you, Klara," he murmured. "I'm so glad we're together in this."

"I'm always with you," Klara replied, putting her arms around his neck. "I chose you, remember?" she teased.

"I believe I chose you," Herman corrected.

"I just let you think that," Klara said impishly, grinning at him.

"I know," Herman said, his eyes softening. "I'm the luckiest man in the world."

"I love you, Herman," Klara whispered. She sat in the circle of his arms for a long time, each one thinking ahead to the times that were to come.

• • •

Alone in her room, Liesel turned from the window and crawled into bed.

"How could they do this to me?" she whispered. She squeezed her eyes shut, and a tear slipped between her eyelids, rolling down her cheek.

Chapter Nine

The next morning, Liesel rose, eyes red from crying, to begin the day. The secret weighed heavily upon her, and she grew angry at the fear that came over her like a dark cloud.

Herman had left for Berlin already, but Klara was waiting for her downstairs.

"Come with me," she said as Liesel walked into the dining room.

"Where are we going?" Liesel asked, following reluctantly.

"You'll see," was Klara's quiet reply.

Klara led Liesel to the back of the house, where no servants worked, and the hallways were quiet. Looking around once, she pressed a small button, hidden in the ornate frame of a painting on the wall. A panel slid open in the wall, and Klara motioned Liesel inside, pulling the panel shut behind them. She clicked on a flashlight and shone the beam around the dark passage.

In spite of herself, Liesel looked around curiously. They were in a room, not too large, but wider than the passage Liesel had used several weeks before. To their left, another passage opened, a little narrower than this one. Ahead of them, the room turned a corner, and Liesel could see no further. To the right, there was a small recess in the wall, with a pile of blankets stacked there.

Liesel took in all of this in a glance, for Klara was already moving deeper into the left-hand passage. Liesel followed her into the passage, watching curiously as Klara pushed a small switch. A second panel slid out of the wall, and Klara pulled it shut. Now they were closed into the left passage, which opened up into a small room.

"Where are we?" Liesel asked.

"Underneath the staircase," Klara replied. "We've actually descended a fair amount due to slight ramps in the rooms."

"Who's going to stay here?" Liesel asked. She helped Klara carry blankets into the room, laying them out on the floor to make rough pallets.

"A family of three, your father said. A man, his wife, and their young son," Klara said. "They'll be arriving in several days."

That night, her sleep was restless, and her dreams filled with Gestapo, who raided the house and took them away to be shot.

"Don't do it!" Liesel cried. "Stop! Please stop!"

She startled awake, breathless and shaking, her sheets soaked with sweat.

The next few days were restless ones for Liesel, as the date of the family's arrival drew closer.

The night they were to arrive, Herman was unable to return to the estate, due to meetings in Berlin.

"What will we do?" Liesel said to Klara, her words becoming panicky.

"Don't worry, Liesel," Klara said. "I'll go collect them myself."

"Be careful, Mother," Liesel whispered.

She watched from her bedroom window as Klara hurried towards the trees bordering the grounds, her blond hair covered by a black scarf.

The night was dark. Clouds obscured the moon and no stars could be seen twinkling above. Klara disappeared into the trees.

Finally, she emerged, followed by two other figures. Liesel ran to meet them at the back entrance, opening the door for them as Klara ushered in a nervous looking couple, the man carrying his young son in his arms.

"Let's go," Klara whispered, leading them to the hidden passage.

She pressed the button and motioned them into the room beyond, shutting the panel behind them. Once inside, Liesel allowed herself to

SUCH A TIME AS THIS

breathe deeply once again. The couple followed Klara silently into the left-hand room.

"I'm sorry it's not much," Klara held out a small bundle to the woman. "Here is bread and butter and apples, and a jug of water."

The woman's eyes filled with tears as she took the bundle. "Thank you. This means everything to us!"

Klara smiled weakly at her in the dim light from the flashlight. "I wish we could do more. Now, I'm afraid you'll have to stay in here until you leave. I'll leave you this flashlight and bring you more food tomorrow night, but you'll have to remain quiet."

"Thank you," the man said gruffly.

"We can never thank you enough," the woman said. "My boy has a chance to live now! To be free!"

Tears glistened in Klara's eyes. "Try to rest. I'll be back tomorrow."

Then, she showed them the small switch to close the panel, and stepped back, waiting for them to close it.

Liesel waited silently, her face a frozen mask of fear. Quickly, made their way back through the passages and climbed the stairs to their bedrooms.

Klara followed Liesel into her bedroom, shutting the door behind them. "Are you all right?" she asked.

"I can't do this," Liesel whispered, nearly choking on the words. "I'm too afraid."

Klara took in her daughter's frightened eyes and trembling hands. "We'll be fine, Liesel," she said, reaching out to hug her. "Don't worry."

"I can't help it," Liesel murmured, her body shaking. "I'm so afraid."

"I know," Klara replied. "But you have to trust that everything will be fine. This is the right thing to do."

Klara led Liesel to the bed, sitting down beside her and smoothing her hair back from her forehead. "Try to sleep."

Liesel lay down, but long after Klara had left, she still trembled violently. In her dreams, the Gestapo dragged her away, screaming.

The next day was an anxious one for Liesel. She jumped nervously at the slightest sounds and roamed the big house restlessly until, finally, Klara suggested that she go to the library and read.

In spite of her worries, Liesel soon found herself lost in a book. The afternoon passed pleasantly, Liesel looking up only as shadows fell across her page. She yawned and stretched, then leapt from the chair as she recalled what nightfall meant.

After dinner, as Liesel readied herself for bed, if not for sleep, a tap on the door startled her.

"It's just me," Klara said as she slipped into Liesel's bedroom.

"I don't think you should come down with me tonight," Klara said. "Just stay here."

"What!" Liesel exclaimed hoarsely.

"I don't want you to be afraid," Klara said.

Liesel was reluctant to concede, yet deep down she was relieved. "All right."

"I'll stop in when I'm back," Klara assured Liesel, and with that, she was gone, flitting lightly down the stairs like a ghost in the night.

Liesel sat down and tried to relax. The minutes dragged as she waited for Klara to return. Liesel closed her eyes, imagining where Klara would be now. She would be downstairs, entering the hidden passage, speaking softly to the Jewish couple. Handing over some food, then explaining where they would be going tomorrow night. Then she would be closing the panel, ducking out of the hidden passage, looking around, coming back up the stairs. Down the hall, and...

Klara knocked on the door and opened it, Liesel sagging in relief.

"Everything's fine," she said.

"When do they leave?" Liesel asked.

"Tomorrow night," Klara replied. "I'll take them to the woods and point them in the right direction."

"All right," Liesel answered.

The next night, Liesel waited anxiously in her bedroom as she watched the small group run into the night. She held her breath as they disappeared into the trees.

Two days of late evenings and sleepless nights had taken their toll on Liesel, however, and her eyelids began to droop as she looked out into the dark night. Her head rested against the window frame as her breathing deepened.

The sound of footsteps in the hall startled Liesel awake.

"I'm fine," Klara said as she entered the room. "They're on their way."

She watched as Klara's eyes misted over.

"What is it, Mother?"

"She hugged me," Klara said. "And said thank you, and I wished that I could have done more. But, Liesel, this makes it all worth it, every heartache, every fear, all worth it."

Liesel lay awake long after Klara had left the room. Her relief that the Jewish couple had left was tempered by the knowledge that this was only the beginning.

• • •

In December, Herman visited with the news that they would have more visitors.

"A young man and his sister," Herman said as they sat in Herman and Klara's bedroom once again, tucked away from any listening ears. "Somehow, they managed to flee from Poland, and they desperately need rest."

"How long?" Klara said, straightening several items on her dressing table.

Herman paused in thought. "I think you should offer them a week," he said. "I'll meet them tonight."

"Tonight!"

"I'm sorry for the short notice," Herman said, "but I have to return to Berlin tomorrow. I could only get away for a day."

"That's fine," Klara said, recovering her composure.

Liesel's heart sank. Her week of unease would begin tonight. A week of restless sleeps filled with nightmares. A week of anxious days, filled with terror of discovery. The feeling of fear came over her once again.

That night, although the meeting came and went without incident, Liesel was not comforted. The Gestapo filled her dreams all throughout that endless week.

Chapter Ten

"Mother, please, can't we stop this?" Liesel pleaded. "We've done our part!"

It was several nights after the Jewish siblings had left to continue on their way. Liesel and Klara sat in Liesel's bedroom, talking quietly.

"No, Liesel," Klara's voice was gentle. "This is the time. Maybe this is why we're here right now. For such a time as this."

"But we've already helped people," Liesel said brokenly. "Isn't that enough?"

"Liesel, do you know how many people are dying?" Klara asked, her voice low. "Thousands of people die *every day* in this war! Life is precious, Liesel! If we can save even one or two, that is worth something! That is why we do this!"

Liesel stared at her mother in shock. She had never seen Klara so passionate about something before.

Klara's face softened.

"Liesel, if it was you, you would want someone to help, wouldn't you?" she said quietly.

"I suppose," Liesel agreed grudgingly, but she wasn't convinced.

• • •

One day, a week before Christmas, Liesel was in the sitting room when she heard a knock on the front door. A maid answered, and Liesel waited to hear who had knocked. As she listened intently, she heard a familiar voice.

"Karl!" Liesel jumped up and ran to the front door.

"Liesel," he said, embracing her. "How are you? It's been so long."

"Fine..." Liesel's voice trailed off as he released her. She froze as she realized all the things she could not tell him.

"I'm fine," she said again, forcing a smile.

"Are you all right?" Karl asked, looking at her intently. "You look pale."

"Yes, I'm fine," Liesel said. "I didn't sleep well last night, that's all." Silently, she prayed that he would believe her.

"I hope you sleep better tonight," he said with concern. "You look like you could use the rest."

"Yes, I'm sure I will," Liesel replied. "Come, join Mother and me for lunch! How long can you stay?"

As they ate, the secrets weighed heavily on Liesel, and her bright chatter and laughter as she spoke to Karl was false. Liesel watched her mother banter with Karl and wondered how she could talk so easily. Every time Liesel spoke to Karl her fear of unintentionally allowing the secret to escape was so strong it threatened to overpower her.

After a good night's sleep, however, Liesel awoke feeling refreshed and relaxed. The events of the past several months no longer threatened to overwhelm her, and she laughed and talked with Karl easily.

That evening, she and Karl sat alone in the library, talking quietly.

"I have something for you," Karl said. "A Christmas present, because I don't know when I'll see you next." He withdrew a small box from his pocket and handed it to her.

Liesel gasped as she lifted the lid. Within it, a delicate gold bracelet lay on a bed of soft white cotton. A tiny sapphire sparkled from the clasp, but aside from that, the bracelet was simple.

"It was my mother's," Karl explained softly. "I wanted to get you something specially made, but with the war..." he shrugged. "Besides, Mother thought you should have it."

"Oh, Karl, it's beautiful!" Liesel said, lifting the bracelet from the box.

"I'm glad you like it," he said.

"Will you put it on me?"

Karl nodded and took it from her hand, clasping it around her slim wrist.

"Merry Christmas, Liesel," he said.

"Merry Christmas, Karl," she replied, taking his hand.

He smiled at her but then looked out the window, towards the city, his eyes narrowed, growing dark and cold. Once again, Liesel felt a flicker of unease coil around her and settle in the pit of her stomach. She watched him, trying to push the unease away, but the feeling remained. Even after their conversation resumed, Liesel couldn't escape the feeling of darkness in his eyes, in his heart.

• • •

Christmas passed, and although Herman did return home, he could only stay for three days.

"Another family will be arriving on the thirtieth," he informed Klara and Liesel. It was December 26, the last day of his visit. Liesel's heart sank at the news. Now, it would begin again, the restless days and sleepless nights, always worrying, always afraid.

The next day, a letter arrived from Karl.

> "*Dear, Liesel,*
>
> "*I am writing to invite you to a small dinner Mother is having on New Year's Eve. She asked if you would come. I hope you will be able to attend with me.*
>
> *If not, please tell your father to inform me when he returns to Berlin. Otherwise, I will pick you up at 6:15.*
>
> *Yours, Karl.*"

Excited at the prospect of a night of fun, Liesel began planning her dress.

"Not too fancy," Klara advised. "This is wartime, after all."

After some deliberation, they decided on a simple, forest green dress, with only the gold bracelet from Karl for jewellery. With some sadness, Liesel recalled her eighteenth birthday. The blue gown still hung, carefully covered, in her wardrobe. She hadn't worn it since, for wartime was no time for frivolities such as luxurious dress or extravagant meals.

The days passed slowly as Liesel waited for New Year's.

On December 30, the Jewish family arrived.

"Liesel, why don't you stay in your room while I go collect them," Klara suggested.

"No," Liesel replied. "I can't sit here waiting. I'll go to the back entrance and wait there."

"Are you sure?"

"Yes," Liesel replied. Her voice was calm, but inside, her fear rose up like a monster, threatening to overwhelm her.

Liesel followed Klara down the back stairs, then watched as she darted across the estate ground, towards the trees. Several anxious moments passed, until Liesel began to regret her decision. Finally, the door opened, Klara ushered in a small group, and Liesel gasped as she found herself face-to-face with a young woman her own age. The young woman's face was dirty and tear-stained, and a deep cut marred her right cheek. Her deep brown eyes, which seemed to bear her heartache, met Liesel's gaze unflinchingly. Liesel could see her suffering, her sadness and pain, and a deep weariness reflected in them.

As Klara ushered them down the back passage, Liesel asked, "What's your name?"

"Helene," the young woman answered.

"I'm Liesel. What happened…" Liesel began to speak, then blushed. "I'm sorry, I shouldn't have asked."

"What happened to my cheek?" Helene said softly.

"Well, yes," Liesel, replied, glancing away.

"I fell," Helene replied. "While running. It got infected, because we've been hiding, trying to get to Switzerland. We hope we'll be safe there."

Liesel took in the dirt on Helene's cheeks and the sorrow in her eyes; she was so young, just like Liesel. In that moment, Liesel finally realized the terrible truth; she understood just how desperate the Jews were to escape.

She shuddered once, then pulled Helene into a hug. "I am so, so sorry."

"It's all right Liesel," Helene said gently. "Look at what you've done," she gestured to the room around them filled with blankets and food.

"But I didn't," Liesel said, feeling tears come to her eyes.

"Liesel, we should go," Klara said, noticing for the first time her daughter's distraught face. "We'll be down tomorrow night," she said to the Jewish couple.

Placing a hand on Liesel's shoulder, Klara led her out of the room, shutting the panel behind them. They climbed the staircase and returned to Liesel's room.

"What's wrong, Liesel?" Klara asked, once they were seated with the door firmly shut.

Liesel buried her head in her hands as tears spilled from her eyes. "I didn't know!" she cried.

"Know what?" Klara asked. She started rubbing Liesel's heaving back.

"I didn't know what was really happening!" Liesel repeated. "I mean, I suppose I knew. You told me. But I didn't *really* know!"

"Ah," Klara said with understanding. "Your heart knows it now, doesn't it?"

"Oh, Mother, how could they do this?" Liesel asked, raising watery eyes to Klara.

"I don't know, Liesel," Klara replied sadly. "This is not the Germany I once knew."

"She will never be mine again!" Liesel said fiercely. "I will never call her my home!"

"I'm sorry, Liesel. I wish I could protect you, keep you safe from all this. But I can't. You have to know, to understand, so that the world may know!" Klara said.

"I was so wrong," she whispered.

Klara left her then, and Liesel sat for a long time, in the silence, thinking of Helene. The Jewish girl had been so kind. How could these horrors be true? How could the government attempt to blot out an entire race of people, without care?

Tears welled up in Liesel's eyes once again at the thought, and she gave herself over to her sobs, crying until her body shook with emotion, and she lay back on her bed, exhausted.

"How can you do this, Germany?" she whispered.

• • •

The next evening, Liesel attended dinner at Karl's house. Maria welcomed her warmly, kissing her on the cheek and teasing her about how much Karl adored her. Liesel blushed and looked for Karl, who she found speaking to his father and several other men.

As they were called to the dining room, Karl returned and offered his arm to her. "I'm sorry," he said. "I was just speaking to them about…"

"The war," Liesel filled in. "I know. It's wretched though! I wish it would end!"

Karl listened indulgently, smiling at her passion, but said nothing.

At dinner, talk centred mainly on the war.

"And how is the SS treating you?" an older man whose name Liesel couldn't recall, asked Karl.

"It's not how it's treating me, but how it's treating the Jews!" Karl replied coarsely.

Liesel forced herself to laugh with the others, but inwardly, she shuddered at Karl's uncaring words. Though conversation continued, the rest of the evening was spoiled for Liesel.

"To 1942!" Karl's father exclaimed as the clock struck midnight.

"To 1942!" the guests chorused, raising their glasses.

"May Germany grow stronger than ever this year!" Friedrich said.

Liesel raised her glass, but her heart rebelled.

Germany is not my home.

After dinner had ended, and the guests had sipped their final cups of coffee, they stood, saying goodbye to Maria and Friedrich. Liesel said goodbye and thanked them for a pleasant evening as Karl helped her into her coat. Together, they walked outside into the crisp winter air.

"Did you enjoy yourself?" Karl asked once they were seated in the car.

"Yes," Liesel replied, forcing a smile.

"I'm glad," Karl said, not seeming to notice her discomfort.

They had only been driving for a moment when Karl suddenly slowed the car and looked intently out the window.

"What's wrong?" Liesel said, trying to see what he was looking at.

Wordlessly, he pointed to the shadows of an alley, and Liesel spotted a figure huddling up against one of the buildings. Karl flashed the headlights on him, and Liesel saw the yellow star upon his chest.

"Hey!" Karl called, rolling down his window. "Come here!"

Liesel glanced over at him, surprised, and saw the figure look up, his eyes widening with terror.

"Come here!" Karl repeated impatiently.

The man stood up, but instead of coming towards them, he began to sprint away in the opposite direction.

Karl pulled out his gun and aimed at the running man. A split second later, Liesel's ears rang from a gunshot, and she screamed.

The man lay crumpled on the ground. Liesel's stomach heaved as she spotted crimson spilling from his chest, illuminated by the car's headlights.

When she ventured a glance at Karl, she shivered at the look in his eyes. They glittered with fanatical intensity, their deep green depths dark and murky. It was then that Liesel saw Karl for who he truly was, how the war had warped him. She opened the car door and heaved the contents of her stomach out onto the street.

"Are you all right?" Karl asked, seeing her distress.

Liesel could only shake her head, unable to speak.

"He won't hurt you," he said. "He's dead now."

Liesel looked at him with horror-filled eyes, hardly believing his lack of understanding, and wondering how she could have ever loved such a cruel man.

"Karl, why?" she whispered.

"Didn't you see the yellow star?" Karl replied briskly. "That man was a Jew. They're a menace." He shook his head. "Haven't you paid any attention to the war? To the Fuhrer?"

Liesel stared at him wide-eyed, horrified at his casual tone.

"I suppose you haven't," he said hastily. "It isn't really for young women to dwell on. Now, let's get you home."

Liesel closed her eyes, blotting out the sight of the dead man. Her mind, however, would not let her forget it.

As they drove, the terrible scene echoed in her mind: the shot, her scream, the crimson blood spilling into the street. Karl's eyes, dark and cold, uncaring, unfeeling. And now they drove away from such cruelty without a backward glance, without a single care for a man whose life had ended because of a murderous whim. Liesel's stomach heaved, and she feared she would throw up once again.

When they arrived at the von Schwarzkopf estate, Liesel climbed numbly from the car with a quiet *goodnight* to Karl.

Upstairs in her bedroom, Liesel sank to the floor, beginning to weep. "How could he do that!" she cried. "That man was innocent! He did nothing wrong!"

She fell asleep that night on the floor, in her forest green dress, spent from weeping uncontrollably.

Chapter Eleven

The next morning, Klara found her lying on the floor. She dropped to her knees beside Liesel's still form, laying a hand on her forehead.

Liesel began to stir, opening her eyes.

"Where am I?" she asked in confusion. All of a sudden, the events of the previous night came rushing back, flooding her mind, and she closed her eyes. Tears slipped from between her eyelids, rolling down her cheeks.

"Liesel, what's wrong?" Klara asked. "Are you all right? Are you sick?"

"No," Liesel cried. "I'm not all right." She began to sob.

"What happened, Liesel?" Klara repeated. "What's wrong?"

"Karl..." Liesel managed to get out.

"Karl?" Klara repeated. "What happened to him?"

"Last night," Liesel said, taking a deep breath to try and calm herself. "He... he... he shot a man last night!"

"Shot a man!"

"Last night," Liesel said brokenly. "On the street! But, Mother, he wasn't doing anything! He was just sitting there! He was innocent!"

"Oh, Liesel," Klara whispered. She gathered Liesel up in her arms, holding her tightly as she wept.

"He told me not to worry, that the man couldn't hurt me anymore, when he saw my face," Liesel said shakily. "But I saw his face first. I saw the darkness there. How could he think that! That man never did anything! He was a Jew, that's all!"

"Liesel..."

"I know now who Karl truly is," Liesel said, her blue eyes stormy. "I will never speak to him again!"

"Liesel, you can't do that," Klara said softly. "He would be suspicious, and because the man was a Jew, no one would take your side if you told them."

"Then what?" Liesel spluttered.

"Give it time, and then break things off quietly," Klara smoothed Liesel's hair back, tucking it behind her ear.

"I don't want to see him ever again," Liesel pushed herself away from Klara and crossed her arms.

"I don't want to see you hurt," Klara said. "I want you safe. Give it a week or two, and then tell him."

Liesel sighed.

"You don't want anything to jeopardize the safety of the Jews that stay here, do you?" Klara said.

"No," Liesel agreed. "I suppose you're right. But I wish I never had to speak to him."

"I know," Klara said. "He's a cruel man. I've seen it in his eyes, but never thought he would do this," she said sorrowfully.

Tears welled up in Liesel's eyes once again. "I can't believe he would do something like this," she whispered.

Seeing that Liesel would not be consoled, Klara stood, and quietly left the room, leaving Liesel to her grief.

Liesel felt as if the weight of the world rested on her slim shoulders. Gone were the carefree days of youth, replaced with the burdens of adulthood. Liesel could not escape the feeling of darkness that hovered over her.

After her tears were spent, Liesel roused herself and got dressed. Lifting her chin proudly, she walked downstairs, resolving to forget about the matter for the day.

"He will not beat me," she muttered. "I will not be controlled by him."

• • •

As night fell on the von Schwarzkopf estate, Liesel prepared to visit the hidden room. She followed Klara down the back staircase and shivered as the chill of the hidden room reached her bones.

"Helene!" Liesel whispered.

The Jewish girl stood from her seat on the floor, leaning against the wooden wall, and walked towards Liesel, a blanket around her shoulders.

"Liesel, how are you tonight?" she asked softly.

"I'm fine," Liesel replied. "I want to apologize, Helene, for two nights ago. I am so sorry! I didn't know!" her words burst from her mouth in a rush, tumbling over each other in their hurry to escape.

"There's nothing to forgive," Helene said gently. "Don't try to carry the weight of the whole world. This isn't your fault, Liesel."

Liesel nodded, but her heart wept for Helene, and the trials every Jew faced. In her mind, she remembered the gunshot, the crimson spilling from the man's battered body.

She held out a small tin to Helene. "I brought some ointment for your cut."

"Thank you," Helene said, taking the tin. "That was kind."

"It's the least I can do," Liesel said, smiling weakly.

All of a sudden, they were interrupted by Klara's quiet voice. "Liesel, we need to go."

"Goodbye, Helene," Liesel said, turning away reluctantly to follow Klara.

"Until tomorrow night," Helene replied, smiling, and Liesel nodded.

Once they were back in Liesel's room, Klara cleared her throat.

"What is it?" Liesel asked, immediately alert.

"It's about Helene," Klara began. "And her family."

"What about them?"

Klara twisted the skirt of her dress, rolling it between her fingers.

"Mother?" Liesel said.

"They're leaving," Klara said, releasing the dress and dropping her hands to her sides. "Tomorrow night."

"What?" Liesel screeched.

"They have to keep going," Klara reminded her. "You knew that. I thought you wanted that."

"Things are different now," Liesel said fiercely. "Things have changed! I've changed!"

"If we truly want them to be safe, Liesel, we have to let them go," Klara said. "They can't stay here forever."

"I know," Liesel replied. "But I want to be friends with Helene!"

"I think you already are," Klara said softly. "And I don't think either one of you will forget the other."

"But that's not the same!" Liesel cried. "It's not the same as talking to each other! As being in the same room!"

"There's nothing I can do to change that," Klara said. "I'm sorry, Liesel, but this is the way it has to be."

"Why is life so hard!" Liesel cried. "It's not fair!" She paced to the window, looking restlessly out of it.

Klara chuckled. "No one said life was fair, Liesel," she said, dropping a kiss on Liesel's head. "Now go to sleep. Goodnight."

"Goodnight," Liesel replied.

Long after Klara had left the room, however, Liesel lay awake.

"First Karl, now this," she whispered to the dark room. "Why?"

But the darkness around her offered no answer, and Liesel fell asleep crying once again.

The next morning, she arose and was brushing her hair when she spotted her jewellery box and had an idea.

"I'll give Helene something," she murmured. "A gift, to remember me by."

She began withdrawing bracelets and rings from the box, laying them on her dressing table. Finally, she picked up a small gold ring intricately engraved and inset with tiny emeralds.

"Perfect!" Liesel ran her finger over the band, watching the emeralds sparkle as the sun caught them. She slipped it onto her finger, to remain there until she could give it to Helene.

Once again, her oblivion tormented her, and she wondered how she could have been so blind. Blind to the fate of the Jews, blind to Karl's cruel heart, blind to Helene's plight. Tears rolled down her cheeks.

"Liesel!" Klara called just then.

Wiping her tears, Liesel left the room. "Yes?" she said as she came down the stairs.

"A telegram just came for you."

"It's from Karl!" she spat as she scanned the paper. "I don't even want to read it!"

"At least see what he has to say," Klara said.

Grudgingly, Liesel unfolded the paper and read. "*Brigitta getting married tomorrow STOP Invited you and me STOP I'll pick you up at 12:30 STOP.*"

"How dare he!" she said, crumpling the telegram in her hand. "What if I don't want to go!"

"Liesel, he doesn't know how you've changed," Klara reminded her. "Only you do."

"I suppose," Liesel said. "But I have to break things off."

"Just remember..." Klara began.

"I know," Liesel interrupted. "I'll be careful."

• • •

That night, Liesel and Klara said goodbye to Helene and her parents.

"Are you ready?" Klara whispered as they entered the room. The flashlight she held made eerie shadows in the darkness.

"We're ready," Helene's father said.

"Helene," Liesel whispered.

"Liesel," Helene murmured. "I'm going to miss you so much!"

"Here," Liesel said. She slipped the ring off of her finger and pressed it into Helene's hand. "So you'll remember me."

Helen lifted the ring, looking at it in the glow of the flashlight. "Liesel, it's beautiful!" Are you sure you want to give it away?" she asked.

"I'm sure," Liesel replied firmly. "I want you to have it."

"Thank you," Helene whispered, pulling Liesel into an embrace. "I will never forget your kindness."

Tears glistened in the girls' eyes as they held each other.

"We need to go," Klara's soft voice interrupted them.

Cautiously, the small group exited the hidden room, with Klara leading and Liesel and Helene bringing up the rear.

At the back door, Liesel embraced Helene once more.

"Safe travels," she whispered.

"Thank you," Helene murmured.

"Thank *you*," Liesel replied.

Liesel watched as the others slipped from the house and darted towards the trees bordering the estate. Klara returned a few moments later, and soon they were each safely back in their bedrooms. Liesel breathed a sigh of relief, but for the first time, it was tinged with sadness.

"If only Helene could have stayed longer," she murmured.

Liesel gazed out her window, craning her neck to try and glimpse the trees where Helene's family was now, but she couldn't. Instead, the lights of Berlin called her attention. Berlin, with the twinkling lights hiding its inner darkness. Liesel's tears fell once again, at the thought of the Jewish man, dead because of Karl's cruelty.

Somewhere in the city, Karl still lived, his actions condoned and encouraged by the evil hearts of those whom Germany called its leaders. And in the streets, the blood of the Jewish man remained, staining Berlin's pristine facade crimson.

"How can they do this?" Liesel wept. "How can they call themselves human, and do this?"

That night, instead of the Gestapo, Karl invaded her dreams, chasing after her with a leering grin, the gun still in his hand. She ran, but could not escape him, nor the crimson that painted her mind red.

• • •

The next day was Brigitta's wedding. Liesel roused herself and climbed wearily out of bed. Sitting down at her dressing table, she sighed at the dark circles surrounding her eyes. She dressed in her pale blue dress with trepidation. Then, she clasped a thin gold chain around her neck and scooped her hair up into a loose twist, held in place with a comb. She was tired of the secrets, tired of being afraid. The thought of seeing Karl made her stomach churn, and she she wished with all her heart that she could avoid it forever, but she was tired of pretending.

When Karl arrived to pick her up, he offered to help her into her coat, but Liesel ignored him, buttoning it up herself.

The journey to Berlin was awkward, far different than their drives of the last several months. Liesel was silent, unwilling to speak with Karl. She stared out the window blankly, wondering how she could stand the drive back to the estate with him. Karl too, was silent. He glanced at Liesel every so often, confused by her silence.

Finally, they arrived at the church. As they waited in the pews, Karl spoke easily with the young man to his left. Liesel sat in miserable silence.

When the music began, the few guests stood and turned in unison to watch Brigitta's entrance. She was dressed in a simple red gown, one that Liesel recognized from a party they had both attended before the war began. Wartime weddings were never fancy, and Brigitta's, for all her grand plans, was no exception.

Her husband-to-be, Kurt, waited at the front. He would be home on leave for only five days, and then would return to the front, leaving his new bride behind.

Liesel tried to keep her gaze on Brigitta, but the sight of her red gown made her stomach churn, as she remembered the Jewish man's blood spilling out onto the street.

The rest of the wedding passed in a blur, until the minister pronounced them husband and wife, and they walked back down the aisle. There would be no reception, only a chance for the guests to congratulate the couple as they left the church.

Liesel and Karl stood together, waiting for their turn to speak to the new couple.

"Congratulations, Brigitta," Liesel said as they reached the front of the line. "I wish you the most happiness."

"Thank you," Brigitta replied, and then she looked between her and Karl slyly. "And when will you be picking a date?"

"Brigitta!" Liesel exclaimed. "We haven't even discussed such a thing," she continued, lowering her voice.

"You'd best be careful, Liesel, or you'll end up an old maid," Brigitta warned.

"I'm not worried," Liesel said.

"I'm just thankful I don't have to worry about such things," Brigitta continued, looking happily at Kurt.

"I'm glad," Liesel said sincerely.

"I bet," Brigitta said with a smirk. "You never did like it when Karl and I spent time together."

"Oh, Brigitta," Liesel said with a laugh. "You know that's not true."

Brigitta tossed her hair and Liesel turned to Karl, who was deep in conversation with Kurt about the front-line troop strength and the SS involvement in various campaigns.

Brigitta cleared her throat.

"Yes, dear?" Kurt said, looking at her.

"We mustn't neglect our other guests," she reminded him.

"Yes, you're right," Kurt agreed, and they bid Liesel and Karl goodbye.

"Nice wedding," Karl said as they walked back to the car.

"Yes, I suppose it was," Liesel agreed bitterly. "It seems Brigitta's gotten the man of her dreams."

Karl glanced quickly at her, surprised at her tone. "I'm sure they'll be happy."

"I would never get married in war," Liesel said.

"Not even to the man you loved?" Karl said, raising his eyebrows.

"I have never loved a man enough to consider it," Liesel drew her arms around herself.

"Not even me?"

"I…" Liesel said quietly. "I need more time. I can't answer that now."

They got into the car, and Karl looked at her, searching her face for something, anything, that might show that she did love him, deep inside. But her dim eyes and downturned mouth showed only sadness and pain, although not for the reasons he imagined.

The rest of the drive passed in silence, Karl too stunned to speak and Liesel too weary to make conversation. By the time they arrived at the estate, Liesel was eager to exit the car and leave the uncomfortable silence behind. She left with a quick goodbye and raced to the front door, closing it behind her without a backwards glance.

Karl sat for long moments, wondering at her strange behaviour. "Probably just the war," he murmured. "I know how she hates it. But still, she's been acting strange lately." He shook his head. "Women!"

He cast another glance toward the house, wondering if, somewhere inside, Liesel watched for him. A curtain flickered, and he smiled smugly. Satisfied with himself, he started the car, and headed down the long driveway, back to Berlin.

Liesel watched from the window as he drove away, remembering his stunned expression, the hurt as he looked at her. Then, she remembered also the gunshot. His eyes as he looked at the Jewish man, lying in the street. In that instant, any pity she had for him disappeared, to be replaced only with a deep sorrow for his cruelty.

"How was the wedding?" Klara's voice startled Liesel out of her thoughts.

"Fine," Liesel replied. "Brigitta seemed happy."

"That's nice," Klara said, but then she shook her head. "Such a shame to be married in war though."

"Her husband goes back to the front in five days. He only got home last night," Liesel said. "Why can't they see what this war does? It tears people apart! Families. Newlyweds. And we gain nothing but death! Death!"

"I know," Klara agreed. "But we can't stop it. We can only hope that those who chose to fight will put a stop to it."

"It's already been almost three years," Liesel moaned, flopping down on to the couch. "How much longer can it go on?"

Klara didn't have an answer, and instead changed the subject. "What did Brigitta wear?"

"A red gown," Liesel replied. "Several years old I think. From before the war."

"Understandable," War is no time for fancy wedding dresses."

"Brigitta always wanted a grand wedding," Liesel said, propping her arm on the back of the couch and resting her chin in her palm.

"She made her choice," Klara sat down next to her on the edge of the cushion. "You can make yours."

"I told Karl I wouldn't get married in war," Liesel said. "And he asked, not even to him?"

"What did you say to him?"

"I told him..." Liesel's voice broke. "I told him that..." Klara laid a gentle hand on her knee. "I told him that I had never loved a man enough to consider it,"

"Oh, Liesel," Klara said.

Liesel scrubbed at the tears forming in her eyes. "I told him I needed time. But time can't take away what he did! Time can't take away who he is..."

"What did he say?" Klara asked quietly.

"Nothing," Liesel said. "He looked at me like he didn't even know me." She sniffled. "Ugh, it seems like all I do is cry. And I hate crying!"

"Oh, Liesel," Klara chuckled. "You'll be all right. You've become so strong."

Klara stood and gave Liesel a pat on the shoulder as she left her alone with her thoughts. Once again, Liesel felt the hurt of Brigitta's barbed comments. Once again, she saw the hurt on Karl's face. Once again, she saw the Jewish man's fear, heard the gunshot, saw the blood, felt his pain.

"Why can't they see?" she murmured.

But again, there was no answer.

Chapter Twelve

A week later, Liesel was reading in the library when the Karl walked in with a bright smile.

"Hello, Liesel."

"Hello, Karl," she replied, setting her book down. "What brings you here?"

"Why so formal?" Karl laughed. "I'm here to see you, what else?"

"Oh," was Liesel's only reply.

Karl frowned and sat down next to her. "What's wrong Liesel?"

"Nothing, really," Liesel replied.

"Is it the war?" he asked. "It'll be over soon. We're going to send them running!"

"The Americans have declared war on us," Liesel said.

"We're Germans, Liesel!" Karl waved his hand. "Victory will be ours! Is that what you're worried about?" he asked. "We're going to win. Don't worry."

Liesel looked at him, knowing she could not say anything more. "I won't," she said finally.

"Good," Karl said, satisfied.

"What have you been doing lately?" Liesel questioned, changing the subject.

"What have I been doing?" Karl repeated with surprise.

"We've never talked about what you do," Liesel defended herself. "I'm curious."

"You don't want to hear about my days," Karl replied. "They're not very interesting," he forced a chuckle.

"I don't mind," Liesel answered.

"This is war Liesel. It's not something a woman should know about," Karl said harshly.

Angry thoughts warred inside of her mind, and she longed to know what he did that he refused to tell her.

She opened her mouth to make a fuming retort, then thought better of it. "I see," Liesel said quietly.

Karl's face softened. "I just want you to be safe," he said, taking her hand. "You know that."

Liesel said nothing, looking down at her hand, enclosed in Karl's. She felt a sudden urge to pull away but forced herself to remain still. They sat in silence until a maid came in, announcing that lunch was ready. Quickly, Liesel stood, grateful for the excuse to remove her hand from Karl's.

Lunch was awkward, made better only by Klara's presence as she managed to draw Liesel and Karl into conversation with her light chatter.

After lunch, Karl excused himself. "What's wrong?" he said as he buttoned up his coat.

"What do you mean?" Liesel replied.

"You've been acting different."

"Different?" Liesel raised an eyebrow.

"Yes," Karl said slowly. "Ever since..." Liesel held her breath, wondering what he was about to say. "The wedding!" Liesel let her breath out. "That's it, you've acted different ever since Brigitta's wedding. Are you jealous?"

Liesel crossed her arms. "What would possibly make you think that!"

"You'd make a good wife," Karl said.

"That's not the point!" Liesel said. "I'm not ready for marriage!"

"Don't you want to get married?" Karl asked, wrinkling his brow.

"Yes," Liesel spluttered. "But not right now!"

"Why not?" Karl asked, looking at her quizzically.

"I'm not ready," Liesel glanced at the floor.

"Why are you so different now?" Karl pulled his coat snug with a sharp tug, doing up the last button with a vengeance.

"Why do you keep pressuring me?" Liesel met his gaze, her eyebrows drawn.

"I'm not!" Karl replied. "You're the one who's changed."

"So what if I have?" Liesel shot back.

Karl sighed. "I'm sorry, Liesel, I don't want to fight with you."

"I don't either," Liesel lifted her face to look into his eyes.

"I should go," he said. "I love you, Liesel." He dipped his head to kiss her cheek, and Liesel held herself stiffly.

"Goodbye, Karl."

He walked out the door, waved once, and shut it behind him. Liesel stood looking out the window, watching as he climbed into his car and drove away Her internal turmoil still raged, and she wondered how she would ever tell him.

"Will he even accept it?" she murmured to herself. "Or will he refuse to believe what I say?"

Yet even as Liesel searched for answers, she couldn't find them. Liesel knew in her heart she must break things off with Karl, that she could never love such a man. And yet she couldn't help but remember the good times they'd shared. The childhood romps. The wild rides, the quiet walks. The dances. The letters. The kisses. Her whole life, she had known him, been with him, grown with him from child to adult.

Now, faced with a crossroads, forced to choose between childhood friendship and newfound truth, Liesel made her decision., But, although she knew her choice was right, it plagued her, and she wished, hoped that she could have both.

In her dreams that night, Karl knocked on the door.

"Where have you hidden the Jews?" he asked. "We know they're here somewhere."

And in her dreams, she led him to Helene. He dragged her away, laughing.

"You can't hide from me, Liesel," he said. "I'll always find out..."

Liesel sat bolt upright in bed, drawing a shaking hand across her forehead. A whimper escaped her lips, and she took several deep breaths, trying to relax.

"It's just a dream," she muttered. "It's just a dream."

Pulling her blankets around her, she closed her eyes and tried to fall back to sleep.

• • •

The next morning, Liesel was braiding her hair when she heard a familiar voice and Klara's happy cry. She ran from her room and down the stairs, spotting Herman at the landing.

"Father!" she cried, throwing her arms around his neck. "I didn't know you were coming home! I've missed you so much!"

Herman chuckled. "I've missed you too."

"We have so much to tell you," Liesel continued, lowering her voice.

"Tonight," Herman promised, giving her a meaningful glance.

Liesel nodded, but she wondered how she could possibly wait that long to tell him everything.

That night, they settled down in Herman and Klara's bedroom. For a brief moment, Liesel remembered the first conversation they had had in secret here. The similarities struck her, as she looked from her parents sitting together on the couch to the fire in the fireplace.

How far they, she, had come. How different her words would be tonight than that first night.

"You were so right," Liesel said.

"About helping the Jews?" Herman raised an eyebrow.

"Yes," Liesel said. "You were so right, but I just couldn't see it!"

"I'm so glad you see it now," Herman said, sinking back in his seat.

"It took Helene to help me see it," Liesel said, leaning forward in her chair.

"Helene?"

"A Jewish girl that stayed with us," Liesel said. "She was my age. She'd been through so much, but she still had so much hope." Liesel took in a deep breath as she steeled herself for the next bit. "And Karl shot a man just because he was a Jew. It was awful! He wasn't even doing anything, but he got scared when Karl called to him, and he ran away."

Herman shook his head. "This is what Germany has become," he said sadly.

"I don't understand. How can people be so awful to each other? Why do they kill for no reason?" Liesel glanced from Herman to Klara and back again.

"All we can do is wait and do what we can to help those who need it," Klara said.

"That's why I came," Herman said. "There's another family coming next week.

"We'll be ready," Klara said, glancing at Liesel.

"Yes, we will," Liesel agreed with a nod.

As she got into bed that night, Liesel thought of her parents. They had been married for over twenty years, and yet, their happiness was as fresh as it was on their wedding day. Liesel felt a lump in her throat as she thought of all they had given up for Germany, and now, for the Jews. And yet, they seemed not to regret anything. She wondered if she would ever find happiness like her parents had.

"Perhaps I will be an old maid after all," she said with a mirthless chuckle, hugging a pillow to her chest.

Chapter Thirteen

April 1942

Spring was coming to the von Schwarzkopf estate. Liesel gazed out the window, looking at the trees, beginning to bud. The grass was still brown from winter, but here and there, Liesel could see patches of green.

The rest of winter had passed in a blur. The days were filled with the everyday tasks that made up their lives. The nights were filled with quiet preparations and hushed journeys, out to the trees and back into the hidden room. The big house was empty, for they no longer had any maids. Now, it was only Klara and Liesel who cared for the house and grounds.

Jews passed through the big house, finding refuge on their way to Switzerland. Liesel listened to their stories, soothed their cuts, sat in silence with those who would not speak.

Karl, too, visited the estate. He and Liesel had several awkward conversations, and yet, Liesel couldn't bring herself to break things off with him.

"What will he say?" she wondered.

One morning, Liesel heard a thud coming from downstairs. She ran down the stairs and stopped in shock at the bottom. Klara lay crumpled on the floor.

"Mother!" she cried, dropping to her knees at Klara's side. "What's happened?"

At the sound of her voice, Klara began to stir and opened her eyes. "What... where am I?" she asked faintly.

"You must have fallen," Liesel replied, laying a soothing hand on Klara's forehead. "You're burning up!" she exclaimed.

"I got dizzy," Klara said weakly. "I must have fainted..."

"I've got to get you to your room," Liesel said. "Can you stand?"

Carefully, Liesel helped Klara to her feet, letting Klara lean heavily on her shoulder. Slowly, they made their way upstairs. When they reached Klara's bedroom, Klara sank back against the pillows at the head of the bed and closed her eyes.

Liesel laid her hand on Klara's forehead, feeling the heat there. "I need water for her fever."

Casting one last glance at Klara's still form, Liesel dashed downstairs. She filled a jug and gathered several cloths, and then made her way back to Klara's bedroom. She set down the jug and dipped a cloth in, laying it on Klara's forehead. Then she dabbed Klara's flushed cheeks with a second cloth. Klara began to shiver, and Liesel pulled the blankets over her, looking at her with concern. Klara moaned, mumbling incoherently.

"What is it, Mother?" Liesel asked, leaning close to try and understand her mother's words.

"Jews... to... night..."

"I know," Liesel soothed.

Klara tried to rise from the bed.

"Lie still," Liesel said, pushing Klara gently back down.

"But... Jews..."

"I know. I'll go get them," Liesel assured her. "Don't worry."

Klara drifted back into delirium, mumbling words incomprehensibly and tossing and turning from the fever. Liesel sat for long hours, bathing Klara's face and neck with cool water and listening to her whimpers. She replaced the blankets when Klara began to shiver and watched as Klara threw them off when she grew too hot.

As night fell, Liesel looked up from her vigil, and stood from her chair at Klara's bedside.

"Wh... where are you going?" Klara asked weakly.

"To get the Jews," Liesel whispered. "Just lie still. I'll be back."

"Be... careful."

"I will," Liesel said, brushing limp strands of hair back from Klara's face.

In the hall, Liesel wound a black scarf over her hair and took a deep breath. She hurried down the stairs, opened the door, and slipped outside. As she hurried away from the house, she heard a rustle of branches.

"What was that?" Liesel murmured. Her heart pounded in her chest, but she forced herself to keep moving.

"It was probably nothing," she whispered, trying to reassure herself. Even as she kept walking, she fought the urge to turn back, to run towards the house, to safety.

A moment later, she entered the trees, grateful for the cover they provided. She glanced around, wondering where the Jewish family was. All of a sudden, they appeared from behind the trees around her. Their clothes were tattered and worn, and their faces were pale with fear.

"Are you the one?" the man whispered hoarsely, stepping towards Liesel.

"Yes," Liesel said, making her voice stronger than she felt. "Follow me."

The man beckoned to his family, a woman clutching a baby and a small boy, about eight years old, and they followed Liesel. She squared her shoulders, determined to be confident for their sake, and stepped forward. For a split second, Liesel remembered her eighteenth birthday, the moment when she had entered the ballroom, and how she had gathered her courage to do so. In the face of what she stepped into now, that moment seemed laughable.

They made their way back to the house, Liesel tense and alert for any sign of danger. At the back entrance, she ushered the Jewish family inside, closing the door tightly behind them.

"Here we are," she whispered as they entered the hidden room. She handed a basket of food to the man, along with a flashlight.

"Thank you," he said softly.

"Yes, thank you," the woman agreed, tears trickling down her cheeks.

"I'm so glad we can help," Liesel replied quietly. "Now," she continued, her tone becoming businesslike. "You'll stay in this inner room. I'll be down tomorrow night to bring more food."

The man nodded as his wife wrapped the baby in a blanket. The young boy stayed close to his mother, watching Liesel with wide eyes.

"I'm Liesel, by the way," she said. The Jewish couple introduced themselves as Hans and Ingrid. Liesel smiled at them, then turned to go.

Liesel went back to her mother's room, and Klara struggled to sit up when she entered.

"Lie down, Mother," Liesel soothed, shutting the door. "It's all right."

"They..." Klara began weakly.

"They're fine," Liesel said. She frowned as she felt Klara's forehead.

Klara slipped back into a restless sleep. A stillness settled over the room, and in the quiet, Liesel could feel her heart beating madly. All alone in the big house, Liesel wished for someone to share her triumph with.

"I did it," she whispered. "I can't believe I really did it."

Even now, the dash into the shadows of the trees seemed far away. Safe now in the bedroom, Liesel felt as if the events of the past several moments were nothing but a dream. As she closed her eyes, the fear that had threatened to choke her rose up still, but smaller now, and was easily overcome by the courage that had carried her through this long night.

Liesel sat long into the night, bathing Klara with cool water. Klara did not awaken, only stirring once or twice. Liesel worked tirelessly with every bit of knowledge she did have.

The sun rose the next morning, and Liesel left her place at Klara's side to stand at the window. The sun crested the horizon, painting the sky pink and orange. Higher up, the promise of a blue sky hung in the air, and dew lay on the grass below.

Liesel looked out upon this scene, yawning. Turning away, she cast a worried glance at Klara's still form, huddled now under the blankets. Wearily, she sat in the chair beside the bed. Soon, her eyes drifted shut, and she slept.

Liesel awoke a short time later to Klara's weak voice.

"Water..." Klara repeated, her eyes still unopened.

Wetting a cloth, Liesel squeezed the cool water gently onto Klara's cracked lips. Feverishly, Klara licked her lips, and Liesel dripped more water into her mouth, until Klara rolled away and accepted no more. Liesel watched her toss and turn with concern.

"What else can I do?" she murmured helplessly.

Suddenly, she realized that she needed to get supplies ready for the Jewish family. After casting an anxious glance toward Klara, Liesel went down to the kitchen, where she gathered bread and butter, apples and water, and wrapped them up. She returned to Klara's bedroom, taking the stairs two at a time. Entering the room, she breathed a sigh of relief to see that Klara had not awoken while she was gone.

"Herman..." Klara mumbled.

"What?" Liesel asked, instantly alert.

"Where... is... he?" Klara murmured deliriously.

"He's in Berlin," Liesel replied. "Remember?"

"Should... be... here..." Klara said faintly.

"He can't leave, Mother," Liesel said. "You know that."

"He has to..."

"Why, Mother?"

"Danger," Klara replied, tossing back and forth. "Danger."

"What danger?" Liesel asked, trying to make sense of her mother's ramblings.

"Danger," Klara repeated feverishly. "Herman... Herman..."

Liesel listened to her moans with growing worry.

"What now?" she murmured, standing up to pace. She walked the length of the room, glancing anxiously at Klara, who continued to toss restlessly.

Going to her, Liesel laid a damp cloth on her forehead, and it seemed to sooth Klara. She settled but continued to mumble confused and jumbled sentences. Occasionally she cried out, startling Liesel, but she never awoke, always slipping back into unconsciousness. As night fell on the estate once again, Liesel laid a hand on Klara's forehead, then pulled away, alarmed at the heat she felt there. Quickly, Liesel placed another cloth on Klara's flushed forehead, hoping desperately that it would bring her fever down. She paced anxiously across the room again, knowing that she must go to the Jewish family, but wanting, needing, to stay with Klara.

"Oh, I wish Father were here!" she cried. "But I have to go."

After laying another cool cloth on Klara's forehead, she hurried from the bedroom, down to the kitchen, and then to the hidden room.

Once inside, she handed the bundle of food to the Jewish woman. "Here you go," she said breathlessly.

"Is something wrong?" Hans asked, becoming alert.

"Wrong?" Liesel repeated. "No. No! You're safe. I promise. It's just..."

"What?" Ingrid asked softly, taking in Liesel's exhausted face, the shadows underneath her blue eyes.

"It's my mother," Liesel said. Her voice broke. "She's sick. Her fever's still rising, and I don't know what to do!"

"It'll be all right, dear," Ingrid said kindly. "Are you sponging her off with cool water?"

"Yes," Liesel replied. "But it's not doing anything!"

"It'll be all right," Ingrid soothed, rubbing Liesel's back. "Just keep doing what you've been doing, Keep her cool. She'll be all right."

"Thank you. I'll be back tomorrow night to see you off," Liesel said.

"That's fine dear," Ingrid nodded. "Go on now."

Impulsively, Liesel reached out to embrace her.

"Thank you," she murmured. A split second later, she turned and was gone, pulling the panel closed behind her.

Before she went back upstairs, Liesel stopped at the kitchen for fresh water. When she got back to her mother's room, she was met with Klara's feverish ravings.

"Herman... not Herman!" she cried. "Please... no... no more! Don't... take us... let... him live! You can't! Please... not Herman! No! No! No!" Klara cried, her voice rising. "No..." she whimpered, settling back into a restless slumber.

Anxiously, Liesel changed the cloth on Klara's forehead. All throughout that long, dark night, Klara's fever rose higher and higher, until she no longer cried out in her delirium, and she tossed and turned in her sleep. Liesel worked tirelessly, replacing the cloths with cool ones. But still, Klara's fever rose, and Liesel began to despair.

"What else can I do?" she murmured, looking down at Klara's flushed face.

Klara's hair, normally sleek and blond, lay matted and damp on her pillow. Her lips were cracked and sweat soaked both her dress and the sheets beneath her. As her fever climbed, she was wracked with chills, and shivered violently.

But as the sun rose over the horizon that morning, Klara's fever broke. Liesel was checking Klara's forehead once again, when suddenly she stopped. For the first time in two days, it was cool to the touch. Klara's breathing had deepened, and she lay still now in a restful sleep that would heal and restore her weakened body.

Liesel let out a long breath in relief and relaxed in her chair. Exhausted, she fell into a deep sleep.

The sun was high in the sky when Liesel awoke to the sound of Klara stirring.

"Wh..." Klara opened her eyes and tried to speak. She swallowed and licked her dry lips. "What happened?"

"You've had a fever," Liesel said. "Oh, Mother, I'm so glad you're all right!"

"Mmm," Klara agreed drowsily. Suddenly, her eyes widened and she tried to sit up. "The Jews!"

"Lie down, Mother," Liesel soothed. "They're fine."

"How?" Klara leaned back against her pillows.

"I went and got them," Liesel replied, sitting on the edge of the bed. "You did?"

"I couldn't leave them!" Liesel exclaimed.

"But I thought you were afraid," Klara said.

"I was," Liesel said quietly.

"Then what changed?" Klara asked.

"I don't know," Liesel said slowly. "I guess I just realized that I needed to grow up. I'm still afraid, but it doesn't rule me now."

"You are so brave," Klara said, reaching over to take Liesel's hand. "Far braver than I am."

"Mother, that is not true!" Liesel squeezed her hand tightly. "You're the bravest person I know!"

"I'm afraid, Liesel," Klara said simply.

Silence fell upon the room as Liesel stared at her mother in shock.

"I'm afraid that I could lose you. That I could lose your father. The only thing that keeps me going is the knowledge that this is right," Klara said.

In that moment, Liesel saw into her mother's heart. Saw her fear, saw her worry, but saw the courage also, a bright spark of bravery that burned fiercely.

"You *are* brave," Liesel said softly. "Courageous."

Klara smiled weakly at her.

"Here, have some water," Liesel said, clearing her throat. "I don't want you to get dehydrated."

"You're a nurse now, are you?" Klara raised her eyebrows.

"I kept you alive, didn't I?" Liesel retorted.

She held a glass of water out to Klara, and then sat back in her chair. Klara drank deeply, then settled back against the pillows. Her eyes were shadowed with exhaustion, and her face was pale.

"Try and sleep, Mother," Liesel said. "You look tired."

"You look tired," Klara replied. "How long have you been awake?"

Liesel wrinkled her brow, remembering. "Two nights," she said finally.

"Without any sleep?"

"I napped once or twice," Liesel replied. "I was worried about you."

"You should be the one sleeping," Klara said. "All I've done for the last two days is sleep."

"You've been sick," Liesel reminded her. "I'll be fine. Don't worry."

At Klara's dubious look, Liesel smiled. "Don't worry!" she repeated. "Here, drink some more water."

"Trying to change the subject?" Klara said.

"I think I liked you better asleep," Liesel teased with a laugh.

Klara rolled her eyes, then closed them. A few moments later, her breathing had deepened, and she slept. The sound of her even breaths lulled Liesel into drowsiness, and soon she too slept. But the uncomfortable sleeping position in the chair eventually woke Liesel, and she stood up, stretching. Dusk had begun to fall, and Klara was stirring.

"I have to take the family out tonight."

"Let me, Liesel," Klara said.

"Not a chance," Liesel said firmly. "You're staying in bed. Besides... I'd like to take them. Really."

"I am so proud of you Liesel," Klara said quietly, and there were tears in her eyes as she spoke.

They sat together, waiting until darkness fell and moonlight bathed the room with a silvery glow. Then, Liesel left the bedroom and walked steadily to the hidden room.

The Jewish family was waiting for her when she opened the panel.

"Ready?" Liesel asked quietly.

"Yes," Hans replied.

As they turned to leave the room, Ingrid unwrapped her baby from the blanket she'd been using.

"Keep it," Liesel said quickly when she saw what Ingrid was doing. "Please."

"Thank you," Ingrid whispered, tucking the blanket back around her baby.

Quietly, they left the house, heading towards the trees. The cool night air drifted over Liesel, and she felt refreshed after taking care of her mother for days without stepping outside.

"Goodbye," Liesel said as they ducked under the trees. "I wish you safe travels. I hope you make it."

"Thank you," Hans said.

"How is your mother?" Ingrid asked.

"Her fever broke this morning," Liesel answered.

"I'm so glad," Ingrid said sincerely. "She'll be fine now, I'm sure."

"We need to go," Hans interrupted.

"Yes, you're right," Ingrid agreed. "Thank you for your kindness," she said to Liesel.

Liesel watched them go deeper into the trees until the darkness swallowed them up. Turning, she moved quickly back across the meadows, towards the house. Although the shadows still hovered in the trees, and the skies were dark above, the fear that had once been so strong in Liesel was gone, replaced by a desire to help those whom she could.

After entering the house, Liesel retrieved blankets from an upstairs closet before going back to her mother's room.

"Did everything go all right?" Klara asked anxiously.

"Everything went fine," Liesel reassured her.

"Good," Klara relaxed back against the pillows. "Why do you have all those blankets?"

"I'm going to sleep in here in case you need anything," Liesel explained, spreading the blankets out onto the floor.

"You don't have to do that," Klara protested.

"I don't mind," Liesel replied. "But I won't sleep in that chair again."

After fixing up her bed for the night, she stretched out on the floor beside the bed, pulling the blankets up to her chin.

"Goodnight."

"Goodnight, Liesel."

Klara watched as Liesel rolled over and promptly fell asleep.

The next morning, Klara tried to get up from bed and dress for the day.

"No," Liesel said firmly. "Stay in bed. I don't want you to get sick again."

"I'm not an invalid, Liesel," Klara grumbled.

"Just stay in bed," Liesel said with a laugh. "I'll be back with breakfast. I'll get you a book to read while you lie here." She grinned at Klara.

Liesel hummed as she worked, slicing bread and buttering it, then placing everything on a tray. She added apples and a few berries, the last of the ones from the previous year's harvest. Then, she headed to the library, selected a book she knew her mother loved, and placed it on the tray.

"Breakfast is served!" Liesel said, as she walked back into her mother's room. She placed the tray down on Klara's lap with a flourish.

"Thank you," Klara said with a smile.

Once they finished breakfast, and Klara was engrossed in her book, Liesel tip-toed out of the room. Back in her own bedroom, Liesel sat down at her dressing table and picked up her hairbrush. She began to brush out the knots from the past two days, pulling the hair smooth once again. As she looked at herself in the mirror, she could scarcely believe that the person who looked back at her had safely hidden four Jews.

I don't feel strong.

But now, the fear that so often accompanied such a thought was gone, replaced with confidence.

I don't feel strong, but I suppose I am.

Liesel lifted her chin, gazing back at her reflection and seeing the determination in her eyes.

I will be strong, she vowed. *Fear won't hold me any longer.*

Chapter Fourteen

"She gets dizzy sometimes," Liesel explained to Herman.

It was May, and Herman had returned to the estate for several days. Klara was in her bedroom, resting, while Herman and Liesel sat together in the library.

"There are very few doctors," Herman said. "Most are with the army or working in the military hospitals."

"What can we do then?" Liesel asked with concern.

"Just keep doing what you've have been. Making her rest. Taking short walks. Talking to her."

Liesel nodded in understanding.

"I'll see if there's any way we can get a doctor, but it doesn't seem likely," Herman shook his head.

"Oh, Father, I was so scared!" Liesel cried. "I didn't know what to do and her fever kept going higher and higher! And I tried and tried, but nothing worked! What if she had died! What if she still does?"

"She didn't, Liesel, and she won't," Herman soothed. "Don't worry. Please."

"All right," Liesel said shakily. "I know you're right," she continued. "But I just imagine what could have happened, and…"

"I know," Herman said softly. "But I'm proud of you."

He smiled and Liesel smiled weakly in return.

• • •

Spring faded into summer as June arrived. Liesel planted that year's garden, carefully sowing carrots, peas, beans, and potatoes while Klara sat nearby, keeping her company, for Liesel would not allow her mother to help. The flowers in the other gardens of the estate were beginning to bloom, and birds flew in the blue skies above. In these moments, the war seemed like a distant memory, a bad dream. But, reminders of war came to the estate again when they heard the sound of a car pulling up to the house.

"I'd better see who that is," Liesel said with a sigh.

She stood, brushing dirt off of her hands, and walked towards the front of the house. As she rounded the corner, she spotted Karl's grey uniform, and her heart sank.

"Liesel!" Karl called as he caught sight of her.

"Hello, Karl," Liesel said stiffly. She turned and walked briskly back to the garden.

"How are you?" he asked, running to catch up with her.

"Fine."

She knelt to begin working again, and Karl looked at her with surprise, taking in her dirtied clothes and hands.

"Have you been gardening?" he laughed. "I never thought I'd see Liesel von Schwarzkopf doing a farmhand's work."

Klara, who had stood and begun to move quietly away, giving the pair privacy, stood stock still at his words. Liesel stood again, her eyes blazing. "This," she said, "is called providing for my family! It is an honourable job and one I do gladly!"

Karl chuckled. "All right Liesel, if you say so."

"How dare you insult me!" Liesel cried angrily. "I chose to do this, and you have no right to come and... and... belittle me!"

"Calm down, Liesel," Karl said, sobering. "I was only teasing. Why are you being like this?"

Suddenly, Klara swayed dizzily.

"Mother!" Liesel exclaimed, ignoring Karl. She rushed to Klara, steadying her.

"Let's get you inside," she said. "I have to go," she glanced back at Karl.

"Liesel, let's talk about this," he pleaded.

"Karl, I don't have time right now!" Liesel kept her arm around Klara's waist as they walked towards the house.

"You don't have time for me?" Karl asked, his eyes widening.

Liesel stopped, turning to look at him. "My mother nearly fainted. I need to help her. That's what families do. Although you don't seem to understand that," she said bitterly.

Turning away from him, she walked into the house without a backward glance.

It was only after she had settled Klara into bed and gone into her own bedroom, that she let her tears fall.

"I must tell him. We can't go on like this. Next time," she vowed.

In the distance, Liesel could hear Karl's car speeding away, but she didn't go to the window to watch him leave.

A few moments later, she wiped her tears away, regaining her composure, and returned to Klara's bedroom.

Klara sat in bed, propped up comfortably against the pillows.

"Are you all right?" she asked with concern as Liesel took a seat beside the bed.

"I'm fine!" Liesel said fiercely.

Klara studied her daughter, taking in her troubled blue eyes. "I'm sorry," she said quietly. "I know how hard this is for you."

"I just wish things didn't always have to change," Liesel complained. "I know that I can't keep seeing Karl, but Mother, he was my friend!"

"I know," Klara squeezed her shoulder. "But you're going to have to tell him sometime. It isn't fair to lead him on."

"Lead him on!" Liesel spread her hands wide. "How could he think I still like him?"

"He's a man," Klara said glibly.

"Just plain dumb, you mean," Liesel grumbled.

"Now, Liesel," Klara reprimanded. "Be nice." But even she could not help smiling.

"I don't want to tell him," Liesel said. "I'm scared of what he'll say."

"You still need to do it," Klara said.

"I know." Liesel's voice was resigned, and Klara couldn't help laughing.

Chapter Fifteen

Two weeks later, Liesel was alone in the library when there was a knock on the front door. She went to the door and answered it, coming face to face with Karl.

"Hello, Liesel," he said. "May I come in?"

"If you'd like to," Liesel said, opening the door slightly. "I was in the library."

Karl followed her into the library, taking a seat in the chair she gestured to.

Liesel sat there in stubborn silence. *If he wants to come to my house and talk, he can start the conversation himself.* She waited, unwilling to speak, and wanting only for him to leave.

"So, Liesel," he began. "How have you been lately?"

Liesel let out a deep breath, admitting to herself one final time that their relationship was over. No more pretending, no more masking her dislike, no more avoiding the fact that their paths had diverged more than Karl could ever know.

"This isn't going to work, Karl," she said.

Karl froze. "What do you mean?" he asked.

"This," Liesel gestured between them. "Us."

"What about us? What do you mean?" Karl pressed.

"This relationship," Liesel said. "It's not working." She looked away, not wanting to meet his eyes, and fidgeted with her dress.

"What do you mean, not working?" Karl moved from his chair to sit next to Liesel and reached out to take her hand. "Sure, we've had some arguments, but that doesn't mean it won't work!"

"We're too different," Liesel said, snatching back her hand and standing.

"We grew up together!" Karl cried. "We did everything together!"

"That's not enough!" Liesel said. "Don't you see? People change! I've changed! So have you!"

"I haven't changed," Karl said bitterly. "You have!"

"I have," Liesel agreed. "That's what growing up is! I've changed, that's true, but so have you."

"I don't know what you're talking about," Karl replied stubbornly, looking away from her.

Liesel swallowed and took a deep breath. "I don't think we should see each other anymore."

"What!"

"We can't," Liesel said, crossing her arms defensively.

"How could you do this to me?" Karl ran his fingers through his hair, messing up his military crew cut. "I thought you loved me!"

"I did, but I told you, people change" Liesel said.

"You've changed, Liesel," he replied coldly. "Not me."

"It won't work!" Liesel cried. "It just can't! I'm sorry."

"Say you love me," Karl pressured. "This can still work."

"No, it can't," Liesel said firmly.

"I'll forgive you," Karl said as he placed his hand on her shoulder.

Liesel shook him off. "You need to leave!" she said, pointing at the door. Her voice was shaky but grew stronger as she spoke.

"You really want that?" Karl said.

"Yes, I do," Liesel said firmly. "It's time for you to go."

Karl glared at her, his gaze filled with hatred and contempt. "I'll go," he snarled. "But you'll wish you had me back!"

He turned then, stomping through the house. The house shuddered from the force of the front door slamming shut.

Liesel sank back into the chair, burying her head in her hands. A single tear slipped between her eyelashes, and she wept for her the freedom of childhood, the carefree days of her youth.

Soon, however, she raised her head, wiping away her tears. She felt as though she could breathe again, as if her burden had been lifted.

Getting to her feet, Liesel left the library, going up the stairs to check on Klara, where she was reading in bed.

"I heard a door slam," Klara said as Liesel sat down next to her. "Is everything all right?"

"Karl was here," Liesel replied. "But everything is fine now."

Klara looked into her eyes, and knew, instantly. "I'm proud of you," she said.

"It was so hard," Liesel confessed. "I didn't think I would be able to convince him! But I told him to go, and he went."

"I'm sorry, Liesel," Klara said finally, reaching over to embrace her.

Liesel leaned into her mother's embrace, drawing strength from it. "Thank you," she murmured.

"Oh, Liesel, I love you so much," Klara said against her hair.

Liesel pulled away. "How are *you* feeling?" she asked with mock sternness.

"Fine, fine," Klara replied.

"Let's go for a walk then," Liesel suggested. "But not for too long."

"Yes, Nurse Liesel," Klara teased, getting up from the bed.

That night, Liesel looked out her window. It was late, and the sky was dark, with only a few stars twinkling above.

"How things have changed," Liesel remarked to herself.

In her mind, she went back, before the war, to that happy summer of 1939. At her birthday ball, when she and Karl had danced, the future had seemed so bright. Now, however, in the clutches of war, the future was uncertain, and capture, followed by death, could come swiftly and without warning.

Liesel sighed, thinking of Karl. His cruelty and coldness. His utter lack of value for Jewish life.

"That might have been me," Liesel whispered, realizing for the first time, and she shivered at the thought.

The memory of his face, furious as he spoke to her, stayed with Liesel as she gazed out the window, into the darkness that surrounded her.

"Oh, Germany," Liesel murmured. "Why do you do this? How can you?"

But there was no answer from the blackness around her. Germany had set her course, with Adolf Hitler at the helm, and onward she charged, onward into darkness.

• • •

The hot summer months passed slowly. June came to a close, and still, Klara swayed dizzily occasionally. Liesel fretted over her mother, urging her to rest and regain her strength.

July was flooded with Jews, fleeing. The hidden room was always occupied, and Liesel made frequent trips into the trees to collect families and bring them to safety in the house. Klara, too, worked, preparing food to offer them and mending old clothes to replace their few tattered rags. In the garden, Liesel weeded and hoed and watered with every bit of strength she possessed, working to ensure a plentiful harvest. In her spare time, she roamed the woods, searching for berries to bring home to Klara, who canned and dried and stored away every bit.

Liesel and Klara fell into a rhythm as they worked alongside one another. The days were full, and at night, Liesel collapsed into bed, sleeping soundly only so she could wake up and do everything over again the next day.

In her busyness, Liesel scarcely had time to ponder her feelings for Karl. It was only in the brief instants of time, as she lay in bed, waiting for sleep, or took a moment to watch the sunrise, that she remembered him, and her heart ached.

Occasionally, she remembered his green eyes, his laughter, his teasing. However, it was the gleam in his eyes as he killed the Jewish man that she remembered most often, and Liesel knew that her decision had been the right one.

Herman visited several times that summer, arriving in a cloud of dust from Berlin. He and Liesel walked and talked, and as they did, Liesel realized once again how much she had missed her father.

August 19, 1942

"I'm sorry we couldn't give you a special birthday," Klara said.

Herman had returned to the estate, and the three of them were sitting outside. A cool breeze blew over them, and in the distance, the sun was sinking lower in the sky.

Liesel opened her eyes, turning to look at Klara. "This is special," she said.

"I know it doesn't compare to your eighteenth," Klara said.

"That was special," Liesel admitted. "But this," she gestured around herself. "This is special too. I love you. There's no one I'd rather spend time with than you two."

"That's exactly how we feel," Herman agreed.

"I've changed," Liesel said slowly. "I used to care about gowns and balls and jewellery, but now I see that people are far more important."

"I'm glad," Herman said.

"And I've seen that in you in the last several months," Klara added. "We're so proud of you."

"Thank you," Liesel murmured, embarrassed.

"Speaking of jewellery, I hope you won't be disappointed by your gift now," Klara said mysteriously. She held out a small box. "This is for you."

"Happy birthday," Herman added, smiling at her.

Liesel lifted the lid of the box, opening it to reveal a gold ring. Within the yellow band lay a single, sparkling diamond, surrounded by intricate engraving. "It's beautiful! She gasped.

"It was mine," Klara said. "My mother gave it to me when I got married. My father gave it to her during their engagement."

Liesel lifted the ring, letting the last rays of sunlight touch the metal, making it gleam. Slipping it onto her first finger, she felt the cool, ageless, metal. "Thank you."

"I'm glad you like it," Klara replied, smiling.

They sat comfortably, until the sun dipped below the horizon, and dusk fell upon the estate.

"Father," Liesel said finally, "When do you think the war will end?"

"I don't know, Liesel," he said. "I don't know."

Klara stood, pulling at Herman's hand. "Let's go inside," she suggested. "It's getting dark."

Herman and Liesel got to their feet, and they walked, side by side, into the house.

Before she went upstairs to her bedroom, Liesel hugged her parents tightly. "I love you so much," she said.

In her bedroom, Liesel ran her finger over the ring's smooth surface. The diamond glittered in the light, shining brilliantly, but outside, the darkness around her seemed to threaten.

Liesel slipped the ring off, clasping it tightly. "I can't let anything happen to this," she whispered.

Glancing over her shoulder, as if to be sure no monsters lurked, she went to the fireplace. Built of stone, the fireplace dominated one wall of her bedroom. No fire was kindled in the hearth now, but in winter, its heat kept Liesel comfortably warm under her blankets. Liesel knelt and tugged at one of the hearth stones, pulling it loose with some effort, to reveal a hidden compartment underneath. Liesel looked at the ring, memorizing its beauty, the engravings, the diamond that sparkled so brightly. Then, she placed it back inside its box, closing the lid and laying the box in the shallow depression. She pushed the stone back in its place so no gap could be seen in the hearth.

Sitting back on her heels, Liesel studied the hearth sadly. "If we had peace," she whispered. "I could wear this. But now, in war... everything has changed. I have to keep it safe."

• • •

The next day, Herman left the estate to return to Berlin.

He hugged Liesel goodbye, holding her tightly. "Take good care of your mother for me," he whispered.

"I will," Liesel promised, looking him in the eye.

He turned to Klara then, taking her hands in his. Suddenly, she swayed, beginning to crumple to the floor. Herman caught her, pulling her close.

"Klara!" he exclaimed. "Are you all right?"

"I'm fine, Herman," Klara said, but she did not let go of him.

Carefully, he ushered her to a bench that sat in the front hall, sitting down beside her, but keeping his arm around her waist.

"Herman, I'm fine," Klara tried to reassure him. "I just got a little dizzy."

"How often does that happen?" he asked with concern.

"Not very often," Klara said.

"How often?"

"About," she hesitated, not meeting his eyes. "Once a week, I think."

"Klara..." he began.

"They don't last long," Klara interrupted him. "I'm fine, Herman," she continued, softening her voice. "Really."

"Please be careful," Herman said. "Don't work too hard."

"I won't!" Klara exclaimed. "Don't worry!"

Herman stood and looked at Liesel. "You'll make sure she doesn't overdo things?"

"I will."

"Herman, I'll be fine," Klara insisted. He hesitated, and she shook her head. "I will!"

"Please be careful," he said quietly.

"I will," Klara reassured him.

"All right," Herman said. "If you're sure."

"I'm sure."

He bent to kiss her, then turned, walking out the door. As he left, Liesel could see the weariness in his step, the weight upon his shoulders, and she wished, desperately, for things to be normal once again.

She turned her gaze to Klara, who shook her head.

"Don't look at me like that," Klara said reproachfully. "I'll be fine."

"All right, Mother, I believe you," Liesel said softly.

"Is something wrong?" Klara asked.

"No," Liesel replied.

But in her mind, a dozen images flashed before her eyes. The bombings on Berlin, the terror, the fear. The night with Karl, when everything had changed. The Jewish man, his lifeless body lying on the street. Helene, and those terrible moments of truth. The worry, and the courage she had sought to carry her through the long, dark nights.

Chapter Sixteen

May 1943

Liesel gazed out the window, thinking of the winter behind them. Not many Jews passed through the house now, for the number of them remaining in the heart of Nazi-occupied Europe was very few.

Spring had come, however, and Liesel continued to hope that this year, 1943, would be the year the war would come to an end. Herman had stayed in Berlin for most of the winter, only returning to the estate for Christmas. Liesel and Klara had done their best to occupy themselves, but the days dragged.

Now, as spring arrived and summer beckoned, Liesel felt her spirits rise. Herman would arrive at the estate the next day, with plans to stay for two or three days, and both Klara and Liesel could scarcely wait. It would soon be time to plant again, and Liesel eagerly looked forward to those long summer days of caring for the garden. In the midst of everything, it seemed as though seemed life had fallen into some semblance of normal.

• • •

The next night, they stayed up late talking, overjoyed that Herman was with them once again. The soft light of the lamps wrapped around them like a comforting blanket.

The clock struck one, and Klara looked up, startled. "My goodness, it's late!"

"We've had so much to catch up on," Liesel said.

All of a sudden, she heard the rumble of car motors outside. "I hear someone coming up the driveway," Liesel said.

Herman leapt to his feet, going to the window. He looked out, straining to see the driveway.

"Gestapo," he breathed. "They've come."

They heard the clatter of boots and banging on the front door. "Open up!" someone yelled. There was a splintering sound as the front door cracked.

"We need to go," Herman said urgently.

"Where?" Liesel cried.

"Just go!" Herman replied.

They heard the sound of men's shouts in the hall, and then the door to the library banged open. Liesel froze. Herman stepped forward, shielding her and Klara. Several men entered the room, hands resting casually on their guns. Their dark coats shadowed their faces, but Liesel didn't have to see to know who they were. She stepped back as Herman reached behind, his hand grasping her arm.

"You will come with us, Herr von Schwarzkopf." A man dressed in black stepped from the shadows of the doorway.

"What have we done?" Herman said, his voice even.

"You have been accused of hiding Jews," the man replied.

"What? Am I not a loyal member of Germany's government?" Herman lifted an eyebrow in surprise.

"That is not for me to decide," the man said. "You may all gather some things, but be quick.

Herman turned towards Liesel and Klara. "Let's go," he said quietly. "Pack extra clothing."

Liesel looked at him, wide-eyed, and opened her mouth to speak.

"Not now Liesel," Herman said softly.

They left the room, the shadowy presence of the Gestapo agents at their backs.

Upstairs, they parted ways, Herman and Klara going to their bedroom, and Liesel going to hers. Alone in her room, with Gestapo agents watching silently from the doorway, Liesel felt icy tendrils of fear creep up her spine. She laid a bag on her bed and went to her wardrobe, look-ing at the dresses that hung there. She moved slowly, mechanically, as she withdrew several dresses: a green long-sleeve, followed by a pale pink and a navy blue short-sleeve dresses.

At her dressing table, Liesel hesitated, looking back at the men who lounged in the doorway, watching her. She picked up a hairbrush and tossed it into her bag. Then, she withdrew two pieces from her jewellery box: the sapphire necklace she had received on her eighteenth birthday and a ring given to her by Herman.

She studied the gold bracelet from Karl, pondering it. Then, suddenly, fiercely, she tossed it aside. It fell, landing in the tangle of objects scattered across the dressing table.

The man in black came to the doorway, followed by Herman and Klara. "We must go now," he said.

Liesel tucked the jewellery into her bag. She began to close it, then stopped, poised in indecision.

"It is time to go," the man repeated.

Liesel whirled to the dresser, where a photograph of her, Klara, and Herman sat. She snatched it and added it to her bag, closing it and grabbing the handle. She fell into step with Herman and Klara.

"Are you all right?" Herman whispered. He was carrying a bag in one hand and holding Klara's hand with the other.

"Yes," Liesel murmured.

As they left the room, Liesel cast a glance towards the fireplace. Beneath the stones, the diamond ring lay hidden from sight.

Will it be safe? Liesel thought. *Did I hide it well enough?* She longed to run back and reclaim the ring, to have it with her and keep it safe, but it was too late.

The Gestapo agents led them outside to the cars waiting on the driveway.

"In here," the man in black said when they reached the second car. Another agent opened the back door, and the family climbed into the back seat, clutching their bags on their laps. The door slammed shut, and they were left alone in the car for a moment. Outside, the man in black conferred with another agent, so quietly that Liesel could not understand a word. Then the front doors opened, and two agents took their seats. The driver started the car, and Liesel looked out the window to see where the man in black had gone. He got into the first car, and it pulled away, with Liesel's car following. As they drove down the road, Liesel looked back towards the house, wondering if she would ever see it again.

• • •

Pressed together in the cramped backseat, the ride to Berlin was not a comfortable one. As Liesel shifted, trying to find a comfortable position, the driver caught her eye in the rear-view mirror, and she stilled, looking down. The fear that she had pushed away for so long, came back now, threatening to choke her with its intensity. She tensed in the seat, closing her eyes, and felt Klara's hand on her arm.

"We're going to be fine," Klara whispered, so quietly that the men in the front did not even look back. "Take a deep breath."

Liesel drew in a deep breath, trying to push back the fear that rose up within her whenever she stole a glance at the silent figures in the front seat.

Eventually, the car slowed and came to a stop in front of a large building.

They were ushered out of the car, and into the building, the man in black leading the way.

A light rain had begun to fall, and water droplets sparkled on the road, reflected in the glow of a single light that shone from the building.

"Gestapo headquarters," Herman muttered, and Liesel felt a shiver of fear go through her.

The man in black stopped at a closed door.

He knocked, and a male voice replied.

"Come in."

The agent in black opened the door to reveal an office, crisp and clean, and behind the desk, a man, clothed in a dark grey suit.

"The von Schwarzkopf family, sir," the agent announced.

"Very good," the seated man replied. "Sit down, please." He gestured to several chairs placed in front of the desk.

They sat, then waited. The agent closed the door and took up a post beside it.

Liesel studied the room. It was clean, almost oddly clean, and unlike other offices she had been in, had nothing on the walls. Aside from the desk and chairs, the room contained no other furniture.

Liesel glanced at the man, then looked down. He had a cold face, she decided. Cold and uncaring. He leaned back in his chair, tapping his fingers together. The silence swelled, until Liesel felt she could bear it no more.

Finally, he spoke. "My name is Heinrich Mueller." At Herman's sharp intake of breath, his eyes gleamed. "I see you've heard of me. Good."

"What do you want from us? We've done nothing," Herman said.

Heinrich leaned forward, resting his arms on the desk. "Nothing, Herr von Schwarzkopf?"

"Nothing."

"That's interesting," Heinrich said, then paused. "Because I spoke to someone who told me otherwise."

Liesel glanced at her mother, her eyes wide. Although she said nothing, Heinrich's keen eyes caught the exchange.

"Perhaps you find that interesting, Fraulein von Schwarzkopf?" he said, turning to Liesel.

"No, sir," she replied, forcing her voice to keep from shaking.

He tapped his fingers again, watching her, until she grew uncomfortable under his gaze.

"You know nothing about hiding Jews," he probed.

"No, sir."

"Nothing about a safe house?"

"No, sir."

"Nothing about a place of rest for Jews who are fleeing?"

Liesel shook her head, hoping that he would believe her.

"Then why," his voice rose. "Why would someone say he was coming to your estate?"

"I don't know, sir," Liesel said.

The man spoke again in a low voice. "Then why, Fraulein, why would a *Jew* speak of a man known only by the name Count?"

Liesel couldn't conceal her involuntary start, and she flinched away from him. Heinrich sensed, if not saw, her surprise and pressed his advantage.

"Why would that Jew tell us of a safe house? A place of protection and rest? A place where he would be met, most likely by a woman, and taken inside, and given food and a place to rest!"

Liesel could feel herself trembling, and she looked down, seeking to avoid his piercing eyes.

He leaned across the desk, moving closer to her. "Perhaps you were that woman, Fraulein?" he turned to Klara. "Or would it be you?"

"And perhaps you," he turned to Herman. "Perhaps you are the man known only as Count? The man who sends Jews to a country estate, to be safe!" he spat.

Liesel could feel tears in the corners of her eyes, and she blinked them back, willing herself not to cry.

"Well, Herr von Schwarzkopf?"

"It's not me," Herman said.

Heinrich rounded his desk and slapped Herman, the sound echoing in Liesel's ears.

"Father!" Liesel cried.

He looked back at her, not speaking, but undefeated. Klara began to weep silently, tears falling from her eyes.

"Perhaps that will teach you to speak truth when you are asked," the man said flatly. "Now, are you the man called Count?"

"I am not."

The man lifted his hand to strike again, this time poised above Klara.

"Don't do it!" Liesel said the words as if they had been ripped from her. "Please!"

He ignored her, looking only at Herman, waiting.

A long moment passed.

"Your time is up," Heinrich said finally, his voice emotionless. Liesel closed her eyes.

"Wait," Herman said.

Heinrich paused. "Are you the Count? I won't ask again."

"I am," Herman replied, looking him directly in the eyes.

"And you've decided to confess to save your wife?" Heinrich sneered. Dropping his hand, he took a seat once again.

Herman didn't reply, merely took hold of Klara's hand.

"And you, Fraulein," Heinrich continued, turning his attention back to Liesel. "It was you and your mother who were the women this Jew spoke of, was it not?"

Liesel darted a glance at Herman, unsure of what to say, and Heinrich took her glance for affirmation.

"I see," he commented, his tone detached. "You, Herr von Schwarzkopf, may have saved your wife from pain now, but perhaps you will wish yourself back once you see the future that lies ahead." He turned his attention to the agent who stood silently by the door. "Escort Herr von Schwarzkopf and his family to a holding cell. Arrange for them to be trucked to Buchenwald tomorrow morning."

"Yes sir."

"No!" Herman cried. "Take me! But spare them! Please, let them go!"

"It's too late for that," Heinrich replied flatly. "Go on now." He sat in his chair, watching as the family was ushered out of the room.

"What is Buchenwald?" Liesel whispered once they were out in the hallway.

Herman merely shook his head. "Not now," he mouthed.

They were led down a long, windowless hallway, with many closed doors on either side, and down a flight of stairs. At the bottom, the man opened a door, motioning for them to enter.

"Go on," he said.

They walked into the cell, clutching their bags, and watched as the door swung shut. A click from the other side provided finality to the terrifying night. Sinking down onto the single, hard bed that lay against one wall, Liesel took in their surroundings as Herman and Klara sat down beside her. They were in a small, windowless room, with bare walls and a dirty pail in one corner, evidently in place of a bathroom. Liesel shuddered. The door was smooth, with no latches on the inside.

"Are you two all right?" Herman asked.

"I think so," Liesel whispered. "But where are we going?"

"A place called Buchenwald," Herman replied.

"But what is it?"

He let out a long breath. "It's a camp," he said. "A place where Jews and people like us go to be contained, out of the way."

"Are we going to die?" Liesel's whispered question hung in the air.

"They won't shoot us," Herman said. "But this camp..."

"It will take all of our courage and strength to survive," Klara spoke for the first time. "But you cannot give up, Liesel!"

"I won't."

"Why don't you two share this bed and try to sleep," Herman suggested.

"I don't think I could," Liesel replied, but she curled up on the bed, trying to relax. Slowly, despite her fear of what lay ahead, her eyes drifted shut, and she slept.

Tiredly, Herman sank to the floor, leaning against the wall for support. Klara sat down beside him, resting her head on his shoulder.

"Thank you for what you did tonight," she said softly. "You didn't need to."

"I couldn't let them hurt you," Herman said, taking her hand in his. "I love you too much."

"I love you too."

"I have to warn you, Klara," he said, "there's a good chance we may be separated. Men and women."

"Oh, Herman, no! Surely not!" Klara clutched at his hand.

"I'm sorry," he replied brokenly. Putting his arms around her, he pulled her close, holding her tightly.

They sat in each other's arms for long moments, silent.

"I'm afraid," Klara whispered eventually.

"I know," Herman murmured. "I am too. But never forget that I love you."

"Oh, Herman, I've always loved you," Klara replied softly. "From the first day I saw you, and all these years have simply made me love you more."

She laid her head on his chest, feeling the steady beat of his heart beneath his shirt, and wondered if this was their last night.

Chapter Seventeen

The next morning came too quickly. The door opened with a bang, startling them awake. Klara jerked upright from where she slept, resting on Herman's shoulder, and Liesel sat bolt upright on the bed.

"What's happening?" she cried, looking at her surroundings with confusion.

Tendrils of blond hair had escaped from her hair pins, and Liesel pushed them carelessly back. Slowly, her disorientation faded, and the events of the previous night came rushing back to her.

"Get up." A voice from the door spoke, startling her. "It's time to go."

Herman got to his feet, assisting Klara while Liesel stood from the bed. The agent at the door tapped his foot as he waited for them. Picking up their bags, they followed him through the building, retracing their steps from the night before.

As they stepped outside, they were greeted by a strong wind that scattered the dust lying on the streets, coating their already rumpled clothing. A truck stood on the street, its driver sitting inside, waiting. The back of the truck was open, with high sides made of wooden slats. Liesel wondered vaguely what this truck was used for, until the agent motioned for them to climb into the back. Shocked, Liesel stood still, looking at him with disbelief.

"Get in," the agent ordered.

"Into... this?" Liesel asked, wrinkling her nose as she looked into the back of the truck.

Herman climbed wearily into the truck, reaching down to help Klara up.

"Get in now," the agent said to Liesel, and something in his eyes warned her not to argue.

Gritting her teeth, she heaved her bag up, then pulled herself up behind it. The agent slammed the back panel shut and walked over to speak to the driver. Peering through the slats, Liesel watched him as he spoke and then retreated inside without a backwards glance. With a rumble, the truck started and began to drive forward.

The next few hours were torturous ones for the family as they huddled together in the back of the truck. The day was windy, blowing dirt into their faces and tangling Liesel and Klara's hair. As the sun rose higher, however, the wind died down and the day became hot.

Several hours into the journey, Liesel began to feel her first pangs of hunger, and she realized she hadn't eaten in many hours. Beads of sweat rolled down her face as the sun blazed down upon them, and Liesel thought wistfully of the garden she would have been preparing to plant now.

Suddenly, Herman's voice interrupted her thoughts. "Liesel."

"Yes?"

"There's something you should know before we get there."

"What is it?" Liesel asked, instantly alert.

"We may be..." he paused, speaking the last words with difficulty. "Separated when we arrive. In fact, it's likely for that to happen."

Liesel stared at him in horror. "No," she whispered. "No more. How much more will there be?"

"I'm sorry," Herman said sadly.

"This is not your fault," Klara said firmly.

"No," Liesel agreed. Tears trickled down her cheeks, dripping slowly onto the bed of the truck.

Leaning back, she covered her face with her hands, willing herself to be brave.

"Be strong, Liesel," Herman said. "We will get through this."

Liesel raised tear-filled eyes to him. "How can we?"

• • •

The hours continued to pass slowly, as the truck carried them over the many miles. Liesel closed her eyes, listening to Herman and Klara's quiet words. The lump in her throat grew larger as she realized what this would mean for them. Opening her eyes, she looked across at them, studying their faces, so familiar for so many years.

Herman looked up, catching her gaze, and patted the spot beside him. "Come over here Liesel," he said quietly.

She did so, feeling tears well up in her eyes once again, and leaned against him.

"I love you," Liesel whispered. "So, so much. Both of you."

"I love you too."

Herman and Klara's response came in unison, and sadness overwhelmed Liesel. Laying her head down on Herman's shoulder, she wept until she felt as if she had no more tears. Herman put an arm around Klara, and the other around Liesel, hugging them tightly.

As the sun began its descent in the blue sky above, the truck slowed. Craning her neck, Liesel peered between the slats of the truck, trying to see where they were. A little way away, she could make out barbed-wire fencing, but apart from that, the slats obscured all other views. A moment later, the truck came to a stop with a lurch, tossing the von Schwarzkopf family down from their seated positions. Sitting back up, they waited nervously to see what would happen next.

All of a sudden, there was a noise at the back of the truck, and the panel opened to reveal several men.

"Out," one ordered. "Now."

Hurriedly, Herman stepped off the back, then turned to help Klara down. Liesel followed, leaping lightly to the ground. Taking a step away from the truck, Liesel looked around and gasped with shock and horror.

Chapter Eighteen

Two days later, Liesel lay in her bunk, trying to get comfortable. Someone down the row groaned, and Liesel felt a tear trickle down her cheek. Across from her, Klara was curled up in a ball, sleeping. Every so often, she tossed restlessly, murmuring in her sleep. Tears stained her cheeks, falling even as she slept.

The stench of unwashed bodies never left the room. Liesel had given up trying to cover her nose.

The thought of Herman, alone on the other side of the camp, brought more tears to Liesel's eyes, and she pressed her hand to her mouth, muffling her tears.

Only a few women shared the low building where they slept, filling the rows of bunks. Each one wore black and white striped pants and a black and white striped shirt, the uniform all camp prisoners were required to wear. Liesel too, wore this clothing, but she could hardly keep from gagging at the thought of how dirty they must be.

Once again, her mind drifted back, two days before, as they had arrived at the camp. Even now, Liesel could scarcely contain her horror at the first sight of the camp. Now, as she lived alongside the same skeleton-like figures she had observed that first day, Liesel wondered if she would soon look the same.

Overall, very few women lived at Buchenwald, and of those, most were waiting to be transported to other camps. Liesel wondered whether she and Klara would be transported away from Buchenwald as well. The thought of even further separation from Herman caused Liesel's tears to begin once again, and this time, she couldn't stop.

She cried herself silently to sleep that night.

The next day dawned dark and gloomy, and Liesel shivered in her thin clothing. After collecting their meagre breakfast portions, the women were assembled outside, and Liesel's fears came true. All the women at Buchenwald were to be shipped to another, smaller camp nearby.

At this news, Klara put her head in her hands. "I can't do it, Liesel," she murmured. "I know I'll never see him again."

"Be strong, Mother," Liesel pleaded. "Don't give up."

Within moments, the women had been loaded into two trucks, pressed tightly together in the cramped space. Liesel put her arm around Klara, keeping her from being jostled in the tightly packed group of women. Klara was silent, appearing not to hear the noise and confusion around her. With deep sorrow, Liesel remembered that terrible moment, two days earlier, when Herman and Klara had been ripped apart. Klara's screams still echoed in Liesel's mind, her cries, pleading with them not to separate them. And then, that last awful moment, as the guards ripped Klara away from Herman, pulling her back, despite her sobs. Klara had collapsed, weeping, against Liesel, who could only watch helplessly as Herman was led away.

"I love you!" he called back, and then he was gone, leaving behind a hollowness nothing else could fill.

Liesel felt tears come to her eyes as she thought of this new, greater separation. As she looked at Klara, her heart ached. The truck bumped across the road, tossing the women from side to side. Above them, the skies seemed to press down, dark and forbidding. Suddenly, they opened, and the rains poured down upon the trucks.

Klara slept curled up against Liesel, who pulled her closer, trying to protect her from the rains that fell now. By the time the trucks pulled up at their new camp, the women were soaked. Liesel's hair had come loose from its tie, and hung plastered to her pale face. Her clothing too, was soaked, but for this, Liesel was grateful, hoping that the rains would wash away the dirt and grime that seemed to be embedded into the very fabric of the clothes.

With a jerk, the trucks came to a halt, jolting Klara out of her slumber.

"What!" she exclaimed. "Where are we? What happened?"

"We're at the new camp," Liesel reminded her.

The panel at the back of the truck creaked open.

"Get out," a voice ordered.

Slowly, the women filed out of the truck, dropping to the ground. Some stumbled as they exited the truck, weak from days and months of camp rations. Just as at Buchenwald, a man sat at a makeshift desk, marking down the numbers on each prisoner's clothing as they exited. For long moments, Liesel and Klara stood silently, waiting for their turn to be recorded. As night fell, Liesel's feet began to ache from standing, and Klara leaned more heavily on Liesel's shoulder. Finally, they were taken to a long, low building, assigned bunks, and left alone. Liesel sank down on her bunk, looking around her. In the dim light, she could see rows of other bunks and the shadowy figures of many women. Klara climbed into bed and fell promptly asleep, exhausted, but Liesel remained wide awake.

"Who are you?" a nearby woman said suddenly, startling Liesel, for she had grown used to the silence.

"Me?" Liesel asked in surprise.

"Yes you! Who are you?" the woman repeated. She sat several feet away on a bottom bunk.

"I'm Liesel."

"Not one of us, are you?" the woman sneered. "How'd you end up here?"

"What do you mean?" Liesel asked, confused.

"You're not Jewish," the woman said simply, as if Liesel was a child. "In fact, you look like a perfect Aryan specimen, from what I can see. Of course, I can't tell if you've got blue eyes, but..."

"I do." Liesel said, surprised to hear herself responding.

"So I'm asking myself what you could have done to get yourself in here," the woman continued as if Liesel had not spoken. "I mean, this certainly isn't a holiday home," she said with a mirthless chuckle, gesturing at the room.

"My family and I..." Liesel's throat felt hoarse. "We were sent here because we were helping the Jews."

Several other women gasped.

"What did you do?" another woman asked quietly.

"We hid them," Liesel answered. "In a secret room in our house."

"Well!" the first woman said in disbelief.

"Don't pay any attention to her," the girl on the bunk beside Liesel whispered.

Liesel smiled tremulously at her, and the girl smiled back. An offering of friendship appeared to have been made, and Liesel accepted it gratefully.

"Is that your mother?" the girl asked quietly, motioning to Klara's sleeping form.

"Yes," Liesel replied softly.

"Is your father at Buchenwald?"

"Yes."

"Mine is too."

"Where's your mother?" Liesel asked.

"She's..." the girl lowered her gaze. "Gone."

"You mean..." Liesel's words trailed off as she glimpsed the girl's stricken face.

The girl nodded, and Liesel reached over, pulling her into her arms, awkwardly due to the slight gap between bunks. "I'm sorry," she whispered.

The young woman said nothing, merely leaned into Liesel's embrace. Tears slipped from between her eyelashes, rolling down her cheeks. Liesel held her, silently, for several moments. The building was quiet, as most of the women had gone to sleep, and Liesel took these moments to study the girl she held. The girl was slightly younger than Liesel, with dark brown, almost black hair falling to her shoulders. She was slight, but as she raised her head, wiping away tears, Liesel could see a spark of determination in her eyes.

"I'm Katrina," she said. "I forgot to introduce myself."

"I'm Liesel."

They smiled faintly at one another, seeing in each other's eyes the spark of friendship, but also a flame of defiance, one that neither of them recognized in themselves.

"We should get to sleep," Katrina said. "They'll put us to work in the morning."

"You're right. Goodnight," Liesel said, laying down on the hard mattress. She fell asleep instantly, exhausted from the long day,

The next morning, after collecting their meagre breakfast portions, Liesel and Klara fell into line with the other women.

"Where are we going?" Liesel whispered, glad to find herself behind Katrina.

"To the factory," Katrina replied.

"Why?"

"To build for the German army," Katrina said. "We make rifles, vehicles, and mortars here. I'm in the vehicle section."

"What do you do?" Liesel asked, curious in spite of herself.

"Put together vehicles for the troops. Not tanks, just vehicles for the regular soldiers."

When they reached the factory, Katrina parted from Liesel, giving her arm a squeeze. "Good luck," she whispered.

Liesel and Klara were left outside with the other new camp arrivals. Finally, a short, balding man came out of the doors, standing in front of the group of women.

"You'll be working here now," he began. "Each of you will be assigned to a section, where you will work from now on."

Liesel and Klara joined the line of women filing towards the door. They each stopped, received their assignments, and disappeared through the doors. Several moments later, Liesel's turn came. Stepping forwards, she waited as the man recorded her uniform number.

"2-6-1-9..." the man finished, muttering. "Name?"

"Liesel von Schwarzkopf."

"Infantry vehicles production," the man grunted, not looking up.

Reluctantly, Liesel stepped away from Klara, entering the building. She walked down the hall, her eyes darting all around her. Wiping her sweaty hands on her uniform, she followed an overhead sign pointing the way to infantry vehicles, and soon she arrived at an enormous room, bustling with activity.

A guard met her at the door.

"New?" he asked.

When Liesel nodded, he pointed towards a small, dark-haired girl.

"She'll show you what to do," he said briskly. "Go on now."

Liesel made her way over to where he pointed. As she approached, the young woman raised her head, and Liesel saw with surprise that it was Katrina. A long, wide table stretched in front of them. As Katrina and the other women in her group finished assembling their part, they slid it across the smooth surface of the table to another woman, who added other parts to the partially assembled structure. Behind them, several women hurried between the rows of tables, passing the partially assembled structures from station to station, where new parts were added on at each one.

"Come here," Katrina said. "I'll show you what to do."

Liesel watched Katrina's hands move swiftly as she assembled parts. Katrina never slowed the pace of her hands, but kept up a running commentary, explaining to Liesel in low voice what she was doing.

"Try it," she said. "You'd better, before someone sees that you aren't working."

"But I don't know what to do!" Liesel protested quietly. "I just started!"

"It doesn't matter," Katrina replied. "I'll help you, don't worry."

Liesel flinched as a woman slid several parts beside her, onto the table. Katrina glanced at her but said nothing. Liesel picked up a partially assembled structure, and pulled another part from the bin beneath the table, trying to imitate Katrina's deft movements in attaching it.

"No, not like that," Katrina said suddenly, pausing in her work. "Turn it. Yes, like that. Now... clip it into place. That's it... and attach this over top," she motioned to a basket of thin metal strips. "Then press it into place... there you go. And slide it across the table."

Liesel did as she was told, pressing the metal strip into place and sliding it across the table. Turning her attention back in front of her, Liesel was stunned to see four more structures waiting for her.

"Things move fast," Katrina warned.

"I see that."

With resignation, Liesel picked up another part, attempting to attach it onto the piece in front of her. As she struggled with it, trying to clip it into place, the part slipped, cutting open a gash on her hand. It promptly began to bleed, and Liesel groaned.

Katrina looked up at the noise and shook her head. "Press it against your uniform," she advised.

"But it'll get bloody," Liesel protested.

"It won't be the first blood on that uniform," Katrina replied, and Liesel pressed her hand wordlessly to her uniform.

Several moments later, Liesel lifted her hand to find that the bleeding had stopped and carefully went back to work.

• • •

By the end of the day, Liesel was exhausted. Her hands were covered with scrapes and cuts, and they had begun to cramp due to the repetitive motions, by the time the supervisor called a halt. Relieved, Liesel stretched and turned to leave.

"Not yet," Katrina warned. "We have to clean the tables first."

A woman came by with a bucket of cleaning solution and rags. Liesel took a rag, wincing at the sting of the cleaning fluid in her cuts. Each woman wiped down their areas and then formed a line to exit the room, dropping the rags in empty pails by the doorway.

Night had fallen by the time they arrived back at the camp. Liesel was so exhausted she just wanted to fall into bed and sleep. But, as she was heading for the barracks, Katrina prodded her in the opposite direction.

"Where are we going?" Liesel asked wearily.

"We have to get our supper," Katrina reminded her. "You'll want it, even if you don't feel like it now."

Liesel nodded, feeling the cramps of hunger in her stomach, and followed Katrina, first to get her supper portion, and then back to their sleeping quarters. Liesel had sunk onto her bunk, choking down bites of her bread when Klara entered. Her shoulders were slumped and her step was weary.

"Mother, are you all right?" Liesel jumped to her feet.

"Yes," Klara said as she sat down on her bunk. "Don't worry."

"What section are you in?" Liesel asked, sitting beside her.

"Mortars," Klara replied. "How was your day?"

"Tiring," Liesel said, lifting a hand weakly. "But I'm fine."

Klara grabbed one of her hands. "Liesel, what's happened?" Klara cried, horrified.

"It's just a few cuts." Liesel tried to brush her mother's concern away.

"Liesel, this is really deep," Klara said, touching the deep gash that ran along the side of Liesel's hand, causing Liesel to flinch.

"I'm sorry, Liesel," Klara said softly.

"I'll be fine, Mother. Really. I promise."

"Be careful," Klara pleaded.

"I'm doing my best," Liesel said. "Really."

As Liesel looked up, she saw Katrina on her bunk, watching them. She caught a shadow of sadness flickering across Katrina's face, and felt a deep sorrow for the other girl.

She hugged Klara tightly, then climbed into her bunk, pulling the single, thin blanket over herself. Liesel closed her eyes. Sleep, however, didn't come easily. She tossed restlessly, images flooding her mind and worries piling up before her. When she finally did fall asleep, terrible dreams plagued her, and she woke panting and afraid.

The gong sounded the next morning, jolting Liesel awake. She pulled herself wearily out of bed to present herself for roll call. The sun was barely peeping over the horizon as she stood, shoulder to shoulder with dozens of other women. Numbers were called, but Liesel could feel herself nodding off. A sharp elbow jabbed at her, forcing her back to attention. Finally, they were ordered into their lines to begin the walk to the factory once again. Inside, Liesel forced her hands to remember the steps of assembly. Slowly, she pieced the parts together, sliding them across the table when she finished.

The cuts on her hands deepened.

At the end of the day, as they walked back to the camp, Liesel flexed her fingers.

"I can't believe how many cuts I have," she said.

"You'll get callouses," Katrina held out her hands for Liesel to see. "I did."

"I hope so," Liesel replied simply.

By the time she had gotten her supper ration and returned to the barracks, Liesel was exhausted. After a murmured goodnight to both Klara and Katrina, she collapsed into bed, asleep within seconds.

The next days and weeks faded into one another, becoming a blur. The gong woke her each morning, starting the long days. Then, the walk to the factory, and the endless hours of assembly, the same motions repeating themselves over and over again.

Finally, the days would end, and Liesel and Katrina would return to the camp, gulping down their supper portions. A quick hug for Klara, a murmured goodnight to Katrina, and Liesel would collapse into bed, sleeping soundly so that she could rise again the next day, only to repeat the actions of the previous day.

The gash in Liesel's hand healed slowly, but her hands still bore faint scars from the cuts. Her hands moved with dexterity now, easily going through the motions of assembly. Liesel's hair had grown, but it hung limp and stringy, streaked with grease and dirt. Each day, she tied it back with a thin strip of fabric she had torn from her bedsheet. The stench of the unwashed bodies all around her no longer bothered her, and she scarcely noticed it, for she had joined their ranks. She had lost weight, and her clothing hung looser than it once had, but her strength had not diminished.

It was Klara that worried Liesel. She too, had lost weight, but with it, Klara seemed to lose her strength as well. She slept heavily each night after walking wearily back to the camp and leaned on Liesel during roll call. Once, Liesel saw her sway dizzily, and she was filled with fear.

"What will I do if something happens to her?" Liesel wondered.

Summer passed, the days monotonous. From gong to bed, Liesel worked, her hands dirty and calloused.

Chapter Nineteen

November 1943

Liesel awoke to the sound of the gong, shivering under her thin blanket. The frosts had come, and the single blanket each woman had did not keep the chill at bay. During roll call, Liesel rubbed her hands briskly together, trying to warm them. She gazed enviously at the guards in their thick winter coats, thinking wistfully of the fur cloak that had once been hers.

For once, she was grateful to get into line and walk to the factory.

"Surely it will be warm there," Liesel said to Katrina.

"Probably," Katrina agreed.

Sure enough, as they entered the large building, they were greeted with warm air.

"Thank goodness," Liesel murmured.

It wasn't warm in the large room where she and Katrina worked, however, because it was too large to heat well. But Liesel soon forgot about the cold as she slipped into the rhythm of assembly.

As she stepped back outside once again at the end of the day, she shivered. The wind had picked up, blowing through Liesel's clothing as if it were nothing. By the time she returned to the barracks, Liesel was glad to climb into her bunk. Pulling her blanket around herself, she tried to get warm. Finally, she drifted off to sleep.

Several days later, she exited the barracks to find snowflakes drifting down from the sky. November passed, the days growing steadily colder.

"I wonder when Christmas is," Liesel remarked to Katrina one day.

"I don't know," Katrina responded. "I've lost track of the days."

"I came here in May," Liesel mused. "But I don't know what day it is now!" she said, growing frustrated. She slammed her palm against her bunk. "I hate this!" Liesel exclaimed fiercely. "I hate not knowing the day! Or the time! Or what's happening outside of our little world!" Her voice broke and she began to sob.

Katrina reached across the gap between the beds, patting Liesel's shoulder, but there was nothing she could say. Eventually, amid the curious stares of the few women who were still awake, Liesel's sobs subsided.

"I'm sorry," she said shakily.

"For what?" Katrina said.

"For crying, and..."

"You think you're the only one who's cried?" Katrina scoffed. "Not even close."

Liesel nodded and tried to smile at Katrina. Her smile, however, did not reach her eyes.

"We should get to sleep," Liesel said quietly.

"Goodnight, Liesel," Katrina whispered.

Liesel laid down on her bunk. She pulled her blanket over her body, but still, she shivered. As she lay there, waiting for sleep to come, the realization of their situation sank in, and panic seized her. *We will never leave here,* Liesel thought. *Not unless Germany loses the war.*

It was this last thought that she focused on, placing her hope in it.

"The Allies have to win," she murmured. "They must."

Realizing she had spoken out loud, Liesel darted a glance around the quiet room, but everyone else appeared to be asleep, not hearing her whispered words.

• • •

Winter passed, and Liesel clung to the hope that the Allies would win the war, defeating Adolf Hitler and the German army once and for all. She dared not speak of this hope to anyone else, not even Klara, for fear one of the guards would overhear. Her hope, however, kept her strong, and the glimmer of courage in her clear blue eyes never faded. She worked and waited, hoping for an Allied victory, but not knowing how she would hear if there was. Nevertheless, Liesel's determination to survive, to overcome, gave her strength to face each day.

"I will not give in," Liesel murmured to herself. Each day, she repeated this, and each day, her resolve grew stronger.

February 1944

Winter dragged on, each day seeming longer than the last day.

With each day, Liesel grew more and more anxious as Klara became only a shadow of her former self. Her cheekbones protruded, the skin stretched over them, and Liesel could feel every bone when she hugged Klara.

"Mother, have some bread," Liesel urged one night, holding out her own portion of bread for Klara to take.

"Liesel, I can't take your food," Klara said, pushing Liesel's hand back weakly. "What will you have then?"

"I'll be fine." Liesel said. "Please, take it."

"No, Liesel," Klara replied. "I won't."

Concern filled Liesel's eyes as she observed her mother. Klara's eyes had lost their clear blue gaze, and she could no longer focus. Her movements were clumsy and her shoulders were continually bowed, as if her body didn't have the strength to hold itself up.

"Go to sleep then," Liesel said softly. "You need your rest."

"So do you," Klara replied.

"I will," Liesel soothed. "Don't worry about me."

Klara laid down in her bunk, pulling the blanket around herself, and closing her eyes. Liesel watched her sleep, the blanket rising and falling with each breath. Klara's frame could no longer be called delicate; she was unhealthily thin now.

Weeks passed, and the first signs of spring arrived. Liesel could hear the occasional twitter of a bird as she walked to the factory and see the first few shoots of grass appearing as the snow melted. As the temperatures rose, Liesel hoped that Klara would recover her strength.

She watched Klara anxiously, hoping to see some improvement, but still, Klara remained weak.

During roll call one April morning, as Liesel was waiting to be dismissed, she felt Klara sag against her shoulder, clutching at her arm for balance. Carefully, so as not to draw the attention of the guards, Liesel held Klara up, steadying her. Finally, they were dismissed, and they fell into line to walk to the factory.

"Mother, are you all right?" Liesel whispered anxiously.

"I... I think so," Klara replied weakly.

"Be careful today," Liesel pleaded. "I'll see you back at camp."

Klara nodded, and they parted ways at the factory doors.

All that day, Liesel could scarcely concentrate. She forced her hands through the motions she knew so well now, but her mind was not on her work.

Finally, the day was over, and Liesel ran back to the barracks. Once there, she looked anxiously around for Klara.

"She's sick," Liesel said worriedly to Katrina. "I know it."

The door opened and a frail figure staggered in. It was Klara. She swayed, and Liesel rushed forward, catching her just before she hit the floor.

"Mother!" Liesel cried. "Come lie down right now!"

"I think I will," Klara murmured faintly.

She leaned heavily on Liesel's arm as Liesel helped her to bed. Laying down, she closed her eyes, drifting off to sleep. Liesel draped the blanket over her thin body, turning to look at Katrina.

"I'm so afraid." Her words were a whisper, so quiet, Katrina had to strain to hear them. "What will I do if something happens to her?"

Katrina squeezed Liesel's hand in comfort, but she had no answer.

The barracks quieted as the women began to fall asleep, but Liesel stayed by Klara's side. She listened as Klara's breaths grew shallow, and her heartbeats faint. Once, Klara's breaths stopped for a split second, and Liesel felt as if her own heart had stopped as well.

As dawn arrived and the barracks began to lighten, Klara stirred. "Liesel..." she said weakly.

"What is it?" Liesel leaned close to her,

With great effort, Klara raised a hand, lifting it to brush Liesel's cheek. "I... love... you," she whispered. "I'm... so... proud... you." Her hand fell from Liesel's cheek, dropping back to rest against the pillow.

"No, Mother!" Liesel cried. "Don't say that! You're going to be fine! Please!"

Clasping Klara's hand in hers, Liesel bowed her head. "Please don't leave me..." she whispered. "You can't go... Please. You'll get better. You have to."

But Klara was silent, and as Liesel raised her head, she saw that Klara's eyes were vacant.

"No!" Liesel cried. "No! Please! No! You can't go!"

Laying her head down on Klara's lifeless body, she wept until her uniform was soaked with tears.

Katrina found her there, still sobbing, when the gong sounded. "Liesel, what's wrong?"

"My... my... my," Liesel could hardly speak, she was crying too hard.

Katrina came closer and caught sight of Klara's still body. "Oh, Liesel! I'm so, so sorry!"

She dropped to her knees beside Liesel and put her arms around her.

"She... she's gone!" Liesel wept.

"I'm so sorry," Katrina murmured. Tears rolled down her face as she held Liesel.

Other women passed, leaving the barracks, and after glimpsing Klara, shot sympathetic glances at Liesel. Eventually, Liesel's sobs subsided.

"I can't believe... she's really gone," Liesel whispered numbly. Her eyes begged Katrina to answer, to have some comfort to offer.

"I know," Katrina said softly. "I know how hard it is..."

"What will I do without her?" Liesel murmured brokenly.

"You'll keep going," Katrina said gently. "For Klara's sake. She wouldn't want you to give up, Liesel."

"What more can they take from me?" Liesel slammed her hand against the bunk. "My father, my mother. My house, my life. Everything... What more will they take?"

Katrina said nothing, but looked anxiously around the barracks. There were only a few women still inside, most had already left to receive their breakfast rations.

"Liesel," Katrina pulled back. "We should go. It's almost time for roll call."

"I can't, Katrina," Liesel shook her head. "I can't go."

"You have to," Katrina said. She got to her feet and helped Liesel up.

With one last glance at Klara's lifeless body, so still on the bunk, Liesel allowed Katrina to lead her away. As she walked through the barracks door, her heart ached, and she bowed her head under the weight of the tears that threatened to spill from her eyes.

Outside, the sun shone brightly for the first time in weeks. Above them, birds swooped through the blue sky, and, through the barbed wire fences of the camp, Liesel could see green grass. This morning, however, Liesel felt only pain at the sight.

"Mother loved spring," she said sadly to Katrina. "And she didn't even get to see it."

That day, at the factory, Liesel couldn't put her mind to the work. The image of Klara, lying alone in the barracks, floated before Liesel's eyes, and she fought back tears.

When they returned to the barracks after collecting their supper rations, Liesel rushed through the door and stopped short.

Klara's body was gone.

"No!"

"What is it?" At the sound of Liesel's cry, Katrina hurried to stand beside her. Her gaze fell to the empty bed. "Oh no."

"They took her!" Liesel cried. "How could they!"

No tears spilled from her eyes now; instead, they were aflame with anger. Katrina watched, stunned, as Liesel ran outside. Then, gathering her wits, she hurried to follow, in time to hear Liesel scream.

"Where did you take her!"

Katrina exited the barracks to see Liesel face to face with a guard, furious.

"Why did you take her?" Liesel repeated.

The guard stared, confused, for a split second, before comprehension dawned on her. "Oh," she said with a cruel laugh. "You're the daughter. Well, she's gone now."

"Where did you take her?" Liesel asked

"She's gone," the guard waved her hand dismissively.

Katrina watched as Liesel opened her mouth, preparing to launch a furious onslaught of words, and ran towards her. "Liesel!" Katrina grabbed Liesel's arm and pulled. "Come with me."

"Yes, go on back to your barracks," the guard agreed, and her eyes were steely as she watched Liesel.

Liesel lifted her chin, determined not to let her tears fall before the guard, and then followed Katrina back to the barracks.

Behind her, Liesel could hear the guard laughing. It was only after Liesel had seated herself on her bunk once again, away from the guard's mocking laughter, that she allowed her tears to fall.

"I didn't even get to say goodbye," she wept. "And I didn't get to see her one last time!"

"I'm sorry, Liesel," Katrina murmured.

Liesel appeared not to have heard Katrina's words. Her thin frame shook with the force of her sobs, and she sat, hunched over on the bunk, consumed with grief.

"It hurts." Katrina sat down beside Liesel.

"So much." Liesel lifted tear-filled eyes to her friend.

Katrina put her arm around Liesel's shoulders. "It always will." She paused. "But tell me something good about your mother, something you and she did together."

She waited, looking at Liesel expectantly, but Liesel glanced away from her intent gaze.

"I don't remember anything!" she cried. "I've been here forever! My life before this feels like a dream sometimes! It feels as if it never existed. Did I ever have a life before this? Before the gong, before the cold, before the loneliness, before Mother faded away to nothing."

There were tears in Katrina's eyes by the time Liesel finished.

"I know." She brushed Liesel's bedraggled hair back from her face. "I watched my mother die too..." She choked back the tears threatening.

"And sometimes I hate them. Hate them for all they've taken from me. Hate them for every day of my life that they're taking even now. But you can't let hate creep into your heart. You can't let bitterness win." She touched Liesel's chin, forcing Liesel to look into her eyes. "Otherwise you'll fade away too."

Liesel drew in a shaky breath. "Before we left our house, my mother and I planted a garden. We talked lots while we worked, and it was really nice." Her eyes filled with new tears, but she tried to smile through them.

Katrina smiled gently at her. "See, you haven't forgotten them all. You'll always have your memories."

"How are you so wise?" Liesel sniffed.

Katrina chuckled in spite of the sadness blanketing them. "Not wise," she said. "Just experienced. When my mother died, someone did the same for me—held me while I cried on these very same bunks and helped me to remember the good things, instead of letting hatred fill my heart."

"So what do you remember about your mother?"

"I remember... how she smiled," Katrina said. "Her eyes always lit up so bright. And I remember how she used to put her finger under my chin and lift it up. She would always tell me to keep my chin up, no matter what happened."

Liesel smiled in spite of herself. "She would have liked my mother."

"I think so," Katrina agreed. She squeezed Liesel's shoulders. "It's okay to be sad, but it's never okay to give up."

"I miss her, Katrina."

"I know," Katrina said softly. "But try to get some sleep."

Mechanically, Liesel laid down, pulling the blanket over her. As she looked across the narrow space between the bunks, she spotted Klara's bunk, empty now, and tears trickled out of her eyes until sleep claimed her.

For days, Liesel grieved. She wept each night, forcing herself to work each day. The sight of her mother's empty bunk brought a searing pain each time she looked at it, and Katrina's words gave her only a little comfort. In these moments, she wondered if her father was dead too, and she was all alone. In the back of her mind, however, the spark of hope refused to be extinguished. It lingered there, fuelling Liesel, waiting to be fully reignited.

A week after Klara's death, a new group of women arrived. When Liesel returned to the barracks that night, she found a strange woman occupying Klara's bunk.

"Oh, Katrina, she's gone!" Liesel cried, weeping with fresh sorrow. She fell into Katrina's arms, clinging to her as she sobbed, while the young woman who now occupied the bunk looked at them with confusion. Eventually, Liesel composed herself and took in the curious gaze of the young woman.

"I'm... sorry," Liesel said shakily. "My mother... she used to have that bunk, but... she's gone now..."

"I'm so sorry," the woman said sincerely, and Liesel held back the flood of tears that threatened to erupt at her simple words.

Chapter Twenty

Spring faded into summer, and Liesel's grief settled in her chest, a deep ache that was with her always. Simple things brought Liesel sadness. The gentle spring rains. The sound of bird song, high above them in the blue sky. The warmth of the first summer days. Each one reminded Liesel of the gaping hole that existed from the loss of her mother.

"I miss her so much," Liesel said sadly.

"You always will," Katrina replied quietly.

It was mid-June, and they were sitting outside the barracks after returning from the factory, eating their supper rations.

"It hurts," Liesel said, pressing her hand to her chest. "Deep inside, it hurts."

"I know."

"I don't even feel like crying anymore," Liesel sighed. "It's just an ache."

"I wonder if we'll ever get out of here," Katrina frowned, deep in thought.

"We will!" Liesel said fiercely. "We have to!"

"I've been here for so long," Katrina said, slumping against the barracks wall.

As Liesel watched her friend who'd endured so much, she felt the flame that lingered deep inside her rekindle. "The Allies will come!" Liesel whispered. "They must!"

"How can you be so sure?" Katrina said quietly.

"Hope," Liesel replied. "It's all I have."

"But..."

"I'm not sure," Liesel said. "But I have to believe they will come. This can't be all that's in store for us."

"You are so brave," Katrina said. "Sometimes I forget what it's like to have hope in the midst of this." She gestured to the camp around them.

"I don't feel brave..." Liesel said, glancing at Katrina in surprise.

"But you are!" Katrina hunched her shoulders. "I was supposed to get married," she said. "But then I was sent here... I don't even know where Joseph is! He could be dead! And I wouldn't even know..."

"I'm so sorry," Liesel reached over and hugged Katrina. Without warning, her thoughts went to Karl, wondering where he was. Wondering if he knew where she had gone.

"I'm so glad you're with me here. I don't know what I'd do without you," Liesel said.

"Me too," Katrina agreed.

Liesel fell asleep easily for the first time that night. She slept deeply, free from nightmares, free from tears, and feeling as if a weight had been lifted from her shoulders.

Chapter Twenty-One

March 1945

Another winter had passed. The snow melted and grass began to carpet the barren ground. The days lengthened, and the monotonous work of the factory continued.

Liesel and Katrina had grown extremely thin over the winter. The long, cold days of hard work had taken their toll on their bodies, and their clothing now hung off of their skeleton-like figures.

They walked slowly, almost shuffling, to and from the factory, and fell heavily into bed each night. One after another, the women around Liesel faded away into death. With each one, Liesel remembered Klara, and her heart ached. Still, however, Liesel's hope never faded. Even as her blue eyes dulled, and she grew weak, the spark of determination never left them.

As April arrived, Liesel continued to give her strength to the factory. The days grew warm, and the walk was no longer uncomfortable. However, even the short walk to the factory drained Liesel's strength. Often, she felt lightheaded and kept her balance only by clutching at a table or bunk.

Suddenly, one day, the atmosphere in the camp changed. Whispers blazed through the camp like a flame.

"The Allies are coming," was the whisper. "The Allies are coming."

Liesel heard the rumours, murmured in her ear, and clutched at them, hoping, desperately, for them to be true.

"Do you think it's true?" Katrina whispered that night.

"I hope so," Liesel replied fervently.

"What if," Katrina hesitated to speak the words. "What if it's not true?"

"Then..." Liesel paused. "We wait."

"For what?"

"For it to be true."

• • •

"Go back to your barracks!" the guard ordered the next morning. Liesel shot Katrina a puzzled glance.

Inside the barracks, the women talked in hushed voices.

"What's going on?"

"Why aren't we going to the factory?"

"What's happening?"

"It is them?"

"Are they coming?"

"Finally?"

"The Allies?" one woman dared to ask.

That night, the air was filled with the sound of guns firing. No one slept. The women huddled together for comfort. All throughout that long night, and the next day, and the next night, they waited, wondering where their futures lay.

Morning dawned, and as the sun rose higher, the guns grew silent. An uneasy quiet fell over the women.

"What's happening?" Katrina whispered.

"I don't know," Liesel replied nervously.

Long moments passed, a tense silence. Finally, they heard the rumble of trucks outside the camp. A woman began to weep.

"They're going to take us away!" she cried. "Away to a different camp! We'll never get out! Never!"

Terrified, Katrina glanced at Liesel, who looked solemnly back at her, unspeaking.

In the silence, they could hear the creak of the camp gates opening. Gunfire sounded close by.

Voices called out in an unfamiliar language. Several shots rang out. Booted feet sounded outside.

Liesel squeezed her eyes shut.

The door opened, and as one, the women looked up to see soldiers in the entrance. Red, white, and blue flashed on the side of the first man's uniform, and Liesel sighed in relief.

"We're safe."

All around her, the women waited in anxious silence. Several soldiers stood frozen in the doorway, their faces stunned. Finally, the first man spoke. Liesel could understand a few words, but most of the women gave blank stares in return. The man beckoned behind him, and a second soldier stepped forward, this one wearing no jacket, only a shirt with the sleeves rolled up.

"Who are you?" he asked, the German words flowing easily from his tongue. "What is this place?"

A moment passed, until finally, Liesel spoke. "It's a camp... for Jews and people the government... doesn't want out in public. Political prisoners."

"The German government put you here?" he asked, his brow wrinkling.

"Yes," Liesel replied.

There was a muffled exclamation from behind him, which the first man quickly silenced. Liesel thought he might be the captain.

"How long have you been here?" the German-speaking soldier asked, horrified.

Liesel tried to count the months in her head. "I... I don't know," she said. "What year is it?"

The man gasped, turning to the captain. A quick exchange passed between them, an outpouring of foreign words.

"April 12, 1945," he told them, switching back to German, and chaos broke out among the women.

Many broke down and wept, clutching at each other for support.

Liesel turned to Katrina, her mind racing. "Two years," she said numbly. "Almost two years."

"Almost three!" Katrina cried, hardly listening. "I've forgotten how long I've truly been here!"

All around them, the women did the same. Their voices rose and fell as women remembered how long they had been prisoners.

• • •

The German-speaking man turned to the captain.

"What are they saying?" the captain asked urgently.

"Some have been here for years," the soldier said. "Three, two. They didn't remember how long they'd been here until I told them the date."

"They need food," the captain snapped. "Let's get them out of here, into the main yard."

"Yes, sir."

He turned back to the women, giving them instructions in German.

The captain watched, anguished, as the women got slowly to their feet, shuffling weakly towards the door. His heart broke for them, and he turned away, calling orders to the men that stood nearby.

• • •

Sam O'Reilly watched the women emerge from the barracks in shock, unable to believe the things he saw now.

"Living dead," he whispered.

He swallowed hard as he watched, and he thought back to his home in Montana. It was peaceful there, and he looked away from the scene before his eyes, an intense longing to return home to the ranch seizing his stomach.

He was here now because his country had called him to fight. The cause was just, but the act made him weary. He had seen such horrors, but this was more awful than anything he had seen before.

He thought of his mother, safely at home on the ranch, tucked away from the reality of war. He hoped she never had to see the things he saw now. It was for her that he fought, he realized anew. Fought so that she would never have to experience the horrors these women had.

Some movement caught the corner of his eye, and he turned to spot a young woman. She was gaunt, as they all were, her bones protruding from her face and hands. Her clothes hung from her thin frame, dirtied and stained, and her blond hair was matted and dull, hardly blond at all now. Chunks had fallen out, leaving bare spots on her scalp, and what remained was pulled carelessly back. He swallowed back the nausea that arose at the sight of her skeleton-like frame, hardly human at all.

She looked, suddenly, into his face, her blue eyes, although dim, still glimmering with a spark of hope and determination. Determined to live, to survive.

He wanted to reach out but didn't know how to, paralyzed by the scenes that would be with him forever.

She dropped her gaze and faded away into the mass of women filling the yard. His heart began to ache, and at that moment, he wished, desperately, to return home. The war he fought had never seemed as long as it did now.

Chapter Twenty-Two

Liesel and Katrina sat leaning against the barracks wall, eating the rations given to them by the American soldiers, the first nourishing food in months, years. Liesel took a bite, savouring the taste.

Suddenly, Liesel sat bolt upright. "My father!" she cried. "Do you think he got rescued too?"

"I don't know," Katrina replied.

"I have to find out!" Liesel cried. She got to her feet, starting towards a group of American soldiers that stood across the yard.

"You go," Katrina said wearily. "I'm too tired."

Liesel slowed for a moment, turning to look at her friend. "Are you all right?" she asked worriedly.

"I'll be fine," Katrina reassured Liesel, waving a hand toward her. "Go on."

Liesel spotted the young man she had seen earlier and walked towards him. "Was Buchenwald captured by the Americans?"

He listened, wrinkling his brow as he mentally translated her rapid words.

"Yes—" he started to say.

"Oh, thank goodness!" she cut him off. "Was there... do you know if a man named Herman von Schwarzkopf was there?"

"I don't know," he said in halting German.

Liesel broke down, sobs shaking her thin body. All the terror and fear, the long nights of worry, the days of hard work, found their release now in her tears, and she wept, unashamed, before him.

He laid a hand awkwardly on her shoulder, and she felt a tentative connection despite the sorrow all around them. "Are you all right?" he asked

Liesel caught her breath, managing to stop her sobs, and looked up at him. "Would you be all right, if you had lived here for two years? If you had had your father ripped away from you without being able to say goodbye? If you had watched your mother get sicker and sicker, and then die? If you had had no way to bury her, but simply came back that night, and found that she was gone? If you had worked your fingers to the bone, for a cause you despised, just to stay alive? Would you be all right?"

The soldier wrinkled his brow, and Liesel could see him trying to understand her words. "I'm sorry," he said. "I didn't think."

Liesel looked away from him. "I'm sorry too," she mumbled. "That was rude of me."

He smiled, and Liesel looked at him, caught in that smile.

"I think you were entitled to it," he said.

"Nevertheless, you are the last person I should be taking this out on," Liesel replied. "I'm sorry."

"Forgiven," he said easily.

Liesel took a deep breath. "I will be all right though," she murmured. "I will."

"You never told me your name," he said.

"You never told me yours," Liesel replied.

"Sam," he held out his hand. "Sam O'Reilly."

"I'm Liesel," she said, shaking his hand. "Liesel von Schwarzkopf."

"Liesel," he repeated, trying the name out.

Her name sounded strange with his foreign accent, but Liesel decided she didn't mind.

Someone called Sam's name from across the camp.

"I need to go," he said. With a nod, he walked away.

She watched him go, towards a group of other soldiers, and studied his appearance.

He was tall, and he stood tall. His uniform was rumpled and dirty, and his brown hair curled around the collar. His face was scruffy, but it was a young man's face, a hint of boyishness still in it. She thought of his eyes, which told of the things he'd seen, the battles he'd been through, the war he fought.

"Sam," Liesel murmured, feeling the unfamiliar word on her lips.

Forcing herself to look away, Liesel made her way slowly back to Katrina.

"What did you find out?" Katrina asked.

"It was rescued by the Americans," Liesel recited. "But he had no idea whether my father was alive or not."

"That's not surprising," Katrina said wearily.

As night fell, the women, returned to the barracks to sleep by force of habit. Liesel did the same, watching from the door as several trucks rumbled away from the camp. Several soldiers guarded the camp perimeter, while the others sat on the ground in the main yard, talking and eating their rations. As the shadows lengthened, however, they fell silent as the darkness closed in around them. The camp had sobered them, just as it would all others who passed through it. Liesel looked out the door before she climbed into her bunk, catching sight of Sam in the fading light.

She went to sleep that night feeling safe and protected for the first time in two years.

The next morning, the American soldiers distributed more food to the starving women. A photographer wandered throughout the camp, among the women, and captured the stark scenes that had been Liesel's life for the past two years.

"I wish Mother could have been here to see this," Liesel sighed as she and Katrina ate their rations.

Katrina nodded. "Where will you go?" she asked. "After this."

"Away from Germany," Liesel said. "She is no longer my home."

"Then to America?" Katrina said.

"I don't know," Liesel said. She fell silent, wondering where she could go, where she could find a home for herself. A place to belong.

Noises from across the camp drew her attention, and Liesel looked up to see a large cluster of soldiers gathered around a man with a highly decorated uniform. The decorated man was standing on a crate of supplies, putting him head and shoulders above the other men, but Liesel could still make out Sam's brown hair among the others.

"I wonder what's happening," she said.

"It looks like something important," Katrina agreed, squinting to try and make out the group more clearly.

"Sam is over there." Liesel kept her gaze fixed on the back of his head.

"So ask him what it's about," Katrina said.

Liesel pulled her eyes away from Sam. "Why would he tell me?"

"I saw how he smiled at you before." Katrina raised her eyebrows, and Liesel shook her head, blushing.

"He was just being nice."

Katrina just smiled.

"They look awfully serious." Liesel cast another glance towards the gathered men.

"Well, I'm sure they're not planning a picnic."

Liesel chuckled, then stopped suddenly. "It feels like so long since I've laughed, truly laughed."

Katrina took a deep breath. "I know. But doesn't it feel like a burden is gone?"

Liesel nodded.

Chapter Twenty-Three

Later that day, Sam found her sitting alone against a solitary tree in the corner of the camp grounds.

"May I join you?" he asked, and Liesel looked up in surprise.

Seeing who it was, she felt a slight smile cross her lips. "Certainly," she replied.

He sat down beside her, his back against the tree, and let out a deep breath.

"How are you?" Liesel asked

"Fine," he replied. He paused. "I want this war to end."

"I know," Liesel murmured. "You don't know how many days I hoped the Allies would come. How many days I hoped that we would be rescued. That hope was the only thing that kept me alive."

He opened his mouth to speak, then closed it again.

"What?" Liesel asked. "Is something wrong?" She paused. "Does it have to do with that meeting you had before?"

He sighed. "I think there's something you should know."

Liesel sat up straight, looking into his eyes, and felt the first stirrings of alarm deep in the pit of her stomach. "What is it?"

"The Soviets are taking over this territory," he said.

"Why won't the Americans stay here?" Liesel asked. She could hear her voice becoming panicky.

"We have to keep going. It's not our territory to keep." he said. "We'll probably leave in a month or two. But my division is leaving in the next few days."

"What will happen to us when the Americans leave?" Liesel

"I don't know," Sam said. His eyes, however, told Liesel all that he did know of the Soviets.

"Look," he said, glancing away from her. "I don't even know why I'm telling you this. I don't even know if I should. I just want you to be safe. To have the chance to create a new life."

"So I should go?" Liesel said tentatively. "But where?"

"Go west," Sam said immediately. "Towards the Americans. You'll be safer there."

"West? But how will I know where to go?"

Sam looked deep into her eyes, ensuring that she paid close attention. "It doesn't matter Liesel," he said. "But if you go west, as far as you possibly can, you'll eventually make it to an American camp."

"And then what?" Liesel wrinkled her forehead.

"And then you'll be safe." Sam swallowed hard. "Trust me, you don't want to get caught here with the Soviets."

"What could they do that the Germans haven't already done to me?" Liesel said doubtfully.

Sam said nothing, merely looked meaningfully at her until her eyes widened with comprehension. A faint blush crept across her cheeks.

"Oh," she mumbled.

"Just get as far away from them as you can," Sam repeated. "I wish I could give you more directions than that, but it's chaos right now. I can't truly say where you'll find help."

"But what if I can't make it?"

"I believe you will."

Liesel studied him for a moment. "Why are you doing this?"

He sighed. "I have seen so much killing, so many people hurting each other. Why? It seems that the only thing I can do to fight against those people, is to help those they would seek to hurt. It's the only thing I *can* do."

"But you're a soldier..." Liesel let her voice trail off. "That's helping. That's real fighting."

He looked at her for a long moment. "Do you think I want to fight and kill, Liesel? Do you think I want to shoot at other young men? They could be my brothers..." he said brokenly. "The only reason I fight is because I know what Germany has done is wrong, and this is the only way to stop them. This is only way I know to prove that good still wins over evil."

Liesel felt tears come to her eyes at his heartfelt words. "Thank you," she whispered. "For everything."

He looked away from her. "Don't thank me," he mumbled. "I haven't done that much."

"Oh," said Liesel, the beginnings of a smile on her lips. "But you have. For me."

Sam got to his feet. "I should go," he said. He hesitated for a moment. "Thank you for listening."

"Of course," Liesel said softly.

• • •

Liesel entered the bunkhouse, blinking her eyes to adjust to the sudden dimness of the building.

"Katrina," she said. "I have to tell you something." She sat down next to Katrina on her bunk.

"What is it?" Katrina lifted anxious eyes to Liesel.

"I was talking to Sam and he said we have to leave."

"But why?" Katrina looked at Liesel, confused. "We've been liberated."

"Sam said the Soviets are taking over this territory, so the Americans have to leave," Liesel said, bouncing slightly on the bed in her urgency.

"The Americans were here first," Katrina protested. "Why should they have to leave?"

"I don't know exactly," Liesel confessed, her eyes clouding. "Sam just said that they have to leave."

"But why do we have to go too?" Katrina frowned. "We're not going with them, are we?"

"Sam said we don't want to get caught with the Soviets." She looked away from Katrina. "Apparently they do bad things to... women... and we have to get away."

"But where can we go?"

Liesel shrugged. "Sam said to go west. He said if we do that, we'll be safer."

Katrina sighed wearily. "I'm so tired Liesel. How can I flee when I barely have enough energy to be here? I can't run." A tear slipped from her eye as she looked at Liesel.

"You have to come." Liesel took Katrina's hand in hers. "You're my friend. I want you with me. I want us both to be safe." She paused. "Besides, I'd miss you terribly if you didn't."

"So you're going, no matter what?"

Liesel looked down at her hands. "I trust Sam. It's strange. I hardly know him, and yet, I believe what he told me. I have to go Katrina."

Katrina sighed. "I suppose I'll come then. I can't very well say good-bye to you now." She looked away. "There's been too many goodbyes already."

Liesel hugged her. "Oh, Katrina, I'm glad!" She sat up straighter. "Now we have to plan what we're going to bring. We should try to save some of our rations the next few days."

Katrina nodded. "And bring the blankets from our bunks."

Liesel smiled faintly. "I'm glad you're coming with me."

• • •

Two days later, Liesel pulled her blanket closed around the few leftovers rations she had managed to save. Beside her, Katrina did the same.

Liesel straightened, looking around the bunkhouse. "I'll be glad to leave this behind," she muttered. Some of the bunks were filled, but many of the women had already stolen away in the night, heading to places unknown. Liesel wondered how many of them would make it to their planned destinations.

A tear slipped from her eye, and she brushed it quickly away, grateful for the dim lighting of the bunkhouse to hide it.

She picked up her bundle and cast one final glance around the building that had been her quarters for over two years.

She touched the rough wood slats of Klara's old bunk as she started for the door. "I wish you could have been here to see this day, Mother," she murmured, blinking back tears.

Taking a deep breath, she turned away and stepped out of the bunkhouse, into the spring sunshine, Katrina close behind her.

"Ready?" she said to Katrina.

"Yes," Katrina replied simply.

Looking around, Liesel spotted Sam, waiting, a little distance away.

"I'll wait here," Katrina spoke before Liesel could. "You go on."

With a grateful glance, Liesel went over to where Sam stood. "Thank you for everything," she said by way of greeting.

"You'll make it," he replied. "Never stop believing that. Just get as far west as you possibly can." He sighed. "I wish I could give you more help."

"I will." Liesel nodded, holding back the tears that threatened to fall. She looked away, brushing away a single tear that had escaped from one blue eye.

"What is it?" Sam asked.

"I feel as though I'm leaving everything I know," Liesel whispered. "Even you. I hardly know you, and I feel as though I'm leaving a dear friend behind."

Sam chuckled. "I'm glad you think of me as a friend."

Liesel sniffed. "It's not very funny. What if I never see you again?"

He started, as if thinking of that possibility for the first time. After thinking for a moment, he withdrew a scrap of paper and a pencil from his uniform pocket. He scrawled several words on it, then handed it to Liesel.

"Sixth Armoured Division," she read aloud, looking at him with furrowed brows.

"It's my division," he said. "That's how you can look for me."

Liesel nodded solemnly. "Auf Wiedersehen."

"Until we meet again," he whispered.

As she and Katrina left the camp grounds, Liesel looked back. Sam stood watching her, and Liesel wondered if she would ever see him again. The feeling of loss overwhelmed her, and a single tear slipped from her eye. Hurriedly, she brushed it away, forcing herself not to dwell on what seemed to be the end of this new friendship.

The two young women walked in silence for most of the day. By nightfall, Liesel was glad to rest, and she and Katrina slept huddled together on the hard ground.

The next morning, they arose, ate a portion of their saved rations, and continued walking. With one eye on the sun, Liesel planned their course, ensuring they were always moving westward. Beside them, barren fields stretched for miles. Bushes lined the dusty road, and Liesel was grateful for the protection they offered from any curious passersby. But, despite her fears, they didn't see another person. As the sun rose higher in the sky during the day, Liesel began to be grateful for the little amount of shade the bushes provided. Although the relief was slight, it was better than nothing, she reflected.

As the sun set, Liesel and Katrina staggered away from the road and slumped at the foot of a stunted tree, exhausted from walking all day.

"Let's keep going," Liesel said.

"Liesel, we need rest!" Katrina said, grabbing Liesel's arm.

Liesel tugged her arm back. "I don't want to stop!"

There was an angry silence as they studied each other. Finally, Liesel let out a deep breath.

"I suppose you're right," she said wearily. She sank wearily to the ground next to Katrina, closing her eyes, and was soon asleep.

The next morning, they shared what little food they had and set out, walking west once again. They were silent, focused on keeping their tired bodies in motion. In their weakened states, every step was a struggle, a fight. But every step carried them away from the impending doom, away from the Soviets that threatened in the east.

The sun rose higher in the sky, beating down upon them. Every muscle in Liesel's body ached, and her stomach cried out for food. Her legs grew heavy, seeming to weigh her down, and she could feel herself begin to slow. Still, they walked onward, always westwards, always moving.

Night fell, and they slept. Morning came, and they walked on.

That afternoon, Katrina perked up. "What was that?" she said. Ahead of them, they could hear a rumble of heavy vehicles coming towards them. A man's shout rose above the clamour of noise.

"Troops," Liesel answered.

They crouched behind some bushes at the side of the road and watched as a group of tanks rumbled past.

"Americans!" Liesel hissed, catching sight of red, white, and blue on the side of the tanks. "We must be getting close."

Her thoughts went to Sam, and she wondered what he was doing now. She closed her eyes, regretting the budding friendship she had been forced to leave behind. The tanks had passed, leaving clouds of dust behind them, and Liesel watched as they faded out of sight, around a bend in the dirt road.

"Let's go," Katrina said wearily, straightening up from her hunched position.

"We must be getting closer," Liesel said quietly.

The next morning, they rose and began following the dirt road. American troops passed at regular intervals, seeming not to notice the pair that trudged along the roadside. At first, the rumble of trucks and tanks startled Liesel, but soon she grew used to the noise, scarcely paying any attention when they passed. She concentrated on putting one foot in front of the other, keeping her body in motion. Every step, however, seemed to take more strength, until Liesel wondered whether she would be able to keep going. Katrina too, grew slower and slower, until the two women were hardly moving at all.

Finally, evening came, and they fell wearily to the ground, too exhausted to eat any of their remaining rations. Katrina was soon asleep, but Liesel remained awake, her mind too active to sleep. She thought of Herman, wondering if he too, had left his camp, and was heading west. Would she ever see him again?

She also wondered if she would ever find Sam again. She put her hand in her uniform pocket, feeling the scrap of paper that rested inside.

"Sixth Armoured Division," she murmured. The whispered words gave her hope, and she clung to it.

"This awful war will not take everything from me," she whispered. "I will find my father, and I will find Sam. Another friendship will not end because of this!"

Chapter Twenty-Four

A week after Katrina and Liesel fled the camp, they arrived at a military camp. The stars on the sides of the tents showed it to be American, and Liesel felt relief surge through her entire body.

"Let's stop here," Katrina suggested.

Wearily, Liesel sank to the ground, mustering her strength to nod in reply to Katrina, who sank down beside her, heaving a deep sigh.

"What now?" she asked, exhaustion filling her voice.

Liesel could only shrug helplessly, unknowing, and too weary to think of a response.

"I suppose we just stay here," she said eventually. "I don't know where else we can go."

Liesel fell asleep instantly that night, on the hard ground outside the American camp.

The next morning, she was startled to see others, dressed in the same tattered uniforms, sitting outside the camp. Each looked the same: the rags of uniforms hanging off their skeletal bodies, the bones protruding, the hollow, empty gaze in their eyes. They sat, waiting for help, yet not knowing where, or when, or if that help would ever arrive. Each one had fled, westward, knowing it was their only chance.

Liesel looked toward the camp. A large manor house dominated one section of the camp, and Liesel realized that they must be on former estate grounds. She swallowed, thinking of her own family's estate, and wondered if it still stood, or if it had been destroyed.

All around the house were clusters of tents, all sporting the American star. Military vehicles were parked haphazardly throughout the camp, and at the outskirts, Liesel could see a group of tanks.

Several soldiers were stationed around the edge of the camp, watching for trouble, and making up for the lack of any physical barrier to protect it.

As the American soldiers emerged from their tents, several came over to the little group.

"Who are you?" one asked. "Where did you come from?"

"From camps," Liesel replied. "In the east. We fled and came west."

Turning to his companion, the man spoke rapidly in an unfamiliar language. Liesel could pick out several words, but apart from that, she simply listened dumbly. Several other soldiers moved through the small group, distributing rations. The portions were small, but Liesel accepted hers gratefully. Eventually, the soldiers moved away, back to their regular duties, and the group was left alone. The noise of the camp flowed around Liesel. She heard it, but did not comprehend the meaning of the noises, for she was too weary to care. Trucks and tanks rumbled through the camp, passing by on their way east, towards the front lines.

That night, Liesel lay awake, thinking of Sam, growing afraid at the thought of him going into battle.

• • •

In his tent that night, Sam thought of Liesel. Liesel von Schwarzkopf. Her name, the only thing he knew of her, and he held onto it, hoping it would be enough. But in his heart, he knew it would take more than a name to find her. Each day, refugees passed them, fleeing west, hundreds of them, always moving.

He wondered if she had made it, moving far enough west so as to escape the Soviets when they came.

There would be battles in the coming days, bloody and fierce, and yet, Sam did not think of them; he thought only of Liesel, wondering if she was safe.

June 1945

The days passed in monotony. More people sat outside the American camp, weak and weary, wondering what would happen to them.

One evening, as Liesel and Katrina were sitting, finishing their supper rations, a group of men, haggard and thin, sat down beside them. One of them jostled Liesel's arm, and she looked up, startled.

"I'm sorry," the man said quietly.

"It's okay," Liesel said simply.

"Klara?"

At the sound of her mother's name, Liesel gasped and turned to look more closely at the man. "Father?"

"Liesel, is that really you?"

"Oh, Father, it is!"

He opened his arms, and Liesel fell into his embrace, beginning to sob. "It's you," she wept. "It's really you."

"I can't believe it's you," he murmured. "But Klara—Where's your mother?"

"She's..." Liesel hesitated, choking back sobs. "Gone."

Liesel watched as tears spilled from her father's eyes. "Gone?" he whispered. "She can't be."

"Oh, Father, I'm so sorry," Liesel cried. "I tried to help her, but... she just got weaker and weaker..." her voice trailed off, and she clung to Herman. "I'm sorry."

He was weeping now, and Liesel held him. Her own tears fell as the loss of Klara hit her once again. They'd lost so much, so many things they couldn't go back to. So much had changed, and Liesel knew she would never be the same. They'd survived the camps, but as Liesel held Herman's shaking body, she wondered if he would survive this new devastation. Her thoughts returned to the cell at Gestapo headquarters, the truck ride to Buchenwald, and she wondered if they had known it would be their last moments together. Klara's screams as the guards had pulled her and Herman apart echoed in Liesel's mind. She knew she would never forget them.

Out of the corner of her eye, Liesel could see Katrina's concerned face as she watched the pair. She stood quietly, watching their reunion, tears running down her cheeks.

"I can't believe she's gone. Really gone."

Herman's trembling voice interrupted Liesel's thoughts, and she wept harder at his words.

"What more can they take?" Herman cried. "Our house, our dignity, our lives as we knew them. Now Klara... What more will they take!" He hunched over, his face in his hands.

Liesel watched helplessly, unable to comfort him, for he mourned Klara far deeper than her. Liesel's loss had mellowed over the last year. The pain was no longer fresh and fierce like Herman's. But, at the sight of Herman's grief, all the sorrow and pain of Klara's death came rushing back. Liesel remembered those last painful moments as Klara had slipped away, weaker and weaker, and tears slid quietly down her cheek. She wept for Klara, and for Herman, for she knew this was a single, last tragedy in the face of the horror they had suffered. Her tears fell on Herman's shoulders, and Liesel knew this would not be the last time they wept together.

"I'm so sorry, Father," she ventured quietly.

"How can I go on without her?" he cried through his tears.

They pulled apart as his tears subsided, studying each other's features. "How did you get here?" he asked shakily.

"We ran," Liesel replied. "My friend Katrina and I—" she gestured to Katrina, still standing beside her. "We ran together, as far west as we could make it, because Sam said the Soviets were coming to our camp."

"Who's Sam?" Herman studied his daughter carefully.

"An American soldier," Liesel said, tucking a loose strand of hair behind her ear. "I've got to find him when this is all over."

"Why's that?"

"I think I've found a friend."

"A friend?" Herman said softly. "Or something more?"

"A friend," Liesel said firmly. She hesitated. "But maybe, someday, something more."

Silence fell on the two as Herman brushed at the tears beneath Liesel's eyes. "I don't want to give you away,"

"You won't have to yet," Liesel said quietly.

"I love you, Liesel," he said suddenly, pulling her to him once again.

"I love you too, Father."

"So Sam told you to go west?" Herman released her.

"Yes," Liesel replied. "He told us we had to leave. So we started walking. We walked for days, and now..." she gestured weakly. "We're here. What about you?"

Herman sighed heavily. "We didn't know for certain if the Soviets were coming, but we heard rumours, so we ran." He gestured to the few other men who sat with him.

"We walked for days too. We lost one of our group... he got too weak and he died."

Liesel felt tears well up in her eyes once more at his story. "Oh, Father," she choked out. "I'm so glad you're here."

"I'm not leaving," he said firmly. "Never again."

Liesel let out a deep breath, letting herself relax, and felt the ache in her chest soften, loosen slightly.

Later that night, Liesel took the time to study her father as he lay on the ground beside her. The camp had aged him. His once brown hair was grey and thinning, with patches falling out in places, and his eyes were haunted and hollow. The father Liesel had once known, strong and teasing, always willing to laugh, to ride, to walk with her, was gone. Herman was a shadow of his former self.

Sadness overwhelmed Liesel as she looked at him. There was so much she wouldn't get back. Klara, the mother she had loved so deeply, the life she had lived, the security, the comfort of her old life. Everything had changed, and she could never go back.

The days passed, slowly, each day a reminder of things past, of things lost, of futures unknown. Still, to Liesel, they were brighter, for her lost father had been found.

"It's strange," Liesel remarked. She was sitting with Herman and Katrina, soaking in the early afternoon sun as they talked. "We're free now. Finally free, from everything. We're not in the camps anymore, we're not behind barbed wire, we're not forced to work every day." She paused. "And yet, we have nowhere to go." She lifted a hand to gesture at the tents around them. "We can't go back. Our old lives don't exist anymore. And so we sit here, waiting... for what?"

"The nightmare has ended." Katrina didn't look at Liesel as she spoke, instead gazing across the camp, watching the soldiers move about. "But there's no dawn to take its place."

"Where do you think we'll go?" Liesel turned to look at Herman. "Father?"

He shrugged. "I suppose we'll have to find somewhere. We can't go home." His eyes clouded. "I imagine Berlin has fallen by now."

Liesel squeezed his hand. "It'll be all right, Father. We'll find somewhere."

"I wonder where I'll go," Katrina said, looking down at her hands.

Liesel's eyes widened. "Katrina! You have to come with us!"

Katrina gestured weakly. "But you have your father back..."

"And you're the sister I never had!" Liesel interrupted. She shifted so that she was looking directly into Katrina's eyes. "We can start a new life together."

Herman looked up from his introspection. "We have to hold tight to the friendships we have," he said. He sighed. "If there's anything we've learned, it's that people can be so easily ripped away from us. Why would we ever let them go of our own free will?"

Katrina's eyes misted over with tears at his words. "You really want me to come with you? Wherever you go?"

Liesel hugged her. "Of course!"

"If Liesel is to have a sister, I suppose that means I'm to have another daughter." Herman laid a hand on Katrina's shoulder, and for a split second, his eyes twinkled, and Liesel caught a glimpse of the man he had been before.

Tears choked her throat, and she hugged Katrina tighter.

As she released her, Liesel caught Herman's eye, and he nodded at her, the faintest of smiles lingering on his lips. Liesel could feel his approval, and she leaned into his embrace, relishing it.

One morning, Liesel was awoken by the sound of tanks entering the camp. The soldiers called greetings to one another, loud and boisterous. Jumping down from their tanks, they filed into the mess tent, emerging a few moments later with rations. A flash of light brown hair caught Liesel's eye, and she looked closely at the group of soldiers, but the man had vanished. A moment later, as the clamour began to die down, Liesel heard a familiar voice.

Standing up from the ground, Liesel scanned the crowd, searching, but not seeing the one she looked for. Disappointed, she looked away, but turned back a split second later, hearing the voice again. The noise, however, soon drowned out the voice she strained to hear.

"Who are these men?" Liesel asked several moments later as a soldier handed her a ration packet.

He looked at her, uncomprehending, then gestured to another soldier to join them.

"Who are these men?" Liesel repeated.

"The Sixth Armoured Division," the man replied, and Liesel's heart leapt.

Could there be a chance, a hope, of another reunion? She had her father back, could she dare hope for more?

"Who are you looking for?" Herman asked, coming to stand behind her.

"Sam," Liesel replied absently.

Several soldiers broke away from the group at the mess tent, heading towards the refugees that lingered on the edge of the camp. Liesel ran to meet them.

"Sam O'Reilly?" she said.

Three men looked blankly back at her, but a fourth jerked his head towards the crowd of soldiers. "That way," he grunted.

Liesel scanned the crowd until she found a familiar mop of brown hair. "Sam!" she called out.

At the sound of his name, Sam turned, searching for the speaker.

"Liesel!" he exclaimed. He ran to meet her, "It's you!" he said as he stopped in front of her.

"My friend," he said softly, taking her hand in his. "I knew you would make it."

Liesel swallowed. "I hoped we'd find each other."

"And here we are." He smiled. "It seems we have gotten something out of this awful mess."

Liesel stifled a giggle. "You're terrible!"

Sam grinned. "Am not." He squeezed her hand. "I hoped we'd find each other too. I didn't want to lose a friend. It seemed awfully unfair at the time."

"My mother used to tell me that life isn't fair," Liesel said, tilting her head back to look into his eyes.

"She was right," Sam shrugged. "But sometimes... there are still happy endings."

Liesel glanced over at Herman, then back to Sam, smiling at him. "I said *Auf Wiedersehen* to you, once, weeks ago," she said. "And I know I'll say it again, but for now..."

"No goodbyes," Sam said. "Only hellos."

• • •

A little distance away, Herman watched them, the tentative smiles they gave one another, the gentleness of Sam's hands as he held Liesel's. He smiled faintly, remembering Liesel's words those few short weeks ago. *A friend... but maybe, someday, something more.*

He looked at them, wondering how long that someday would take to arrive, and thought of Klara. Tears welled up in his eyes once again, and he let them fall unashamedly. Liesel had grown up. His little girl was a woman now, and the thought saddened him.

He had missed out on so much, but now, watching Liesel's smile, and seeing the sparkle reappear in her eyes, he knew they hadn't lost everything.

"Today the guns are silent. A great tragedy has ended. A great victory has been won. The skies no longer rain death—the seas bear only commerce—men everywhere walk upright in the sunlight. The entire world is quietly at peace."—General Douglas MacArthur

"...and men will still say, 'This was their finest hour.'"—Winston Churchill

Epilogue

Saturday, April 12, 1947

They married two years later in a little church in Sam's hometown, the pews filled with their closest friends. Flowers decorated the aisle, filling the church with their sweet smell.

At the front, Sam waited for her. Beside him stood his brother, and across from them, Katrina stood tall and straight. She clutched a bouquet of flowers tightly, and she smiled as she watched Liesel come down the aisle.

Liesel's dress was simple, but elegant, with long, lacy sleeves. Her cheeks were flushed with excitement, their colour vivid against the crisp white of the dress, and she held tightly to a bouquet of wildflowers in one hand. With the other hand, she clutched Herman's arm as he walked her down the aisle, the music floating around them. She kept her eyes on Sam as she walked towards him, captured by the wonder and love she saw in his gaze.

"Hello, my friend," he mouthed as she reached the altar.

"I love you, my friend," she mouthed back, letting her smile bloom across her face.

Herman kissed her cheek as he released her, and she took Sam's hands as she took her place next to him.

"No more goodbyes," Sam replied.

Tears glittered in Liesel's eyes. Tears for the past, the mother she mourned so deeply, the father she would now leave to join with another.

Tears for the life she had known, the pain, the suffering of those long years. But she knew those days were gone, fading in the glow of the present, never to be forgotten.

Liesel looked at Sam's hands in hers. She remembered his gaze, his pity, his pain. Remembered the warrior, who was still a man in the midst of horror, and loved him all the more for it. Now, as they looked into each other's eyes, it seemed that their entire lives lay ahead of them, so bright with new hope.

9 781486 620678